Joseph Tuckerman

A Memorial of Rev. Joseph Tuckerman

Joseph Tuckerman

A Memorial of Rev. Joseph Tuckerman

ISBN/EAN: 9783337424329

Printed in Europe, USA, Canada, Australia, Japan

Cover: Foto ©Raphael Reischuk / pixelio.de

More available books at **www.hansebooks.com**

Rev. JOSEPH TUCKERMAN.

WORCESTER, MASSACHUSETTS:

1888.

CONTENTS.

BIOGRAPHICAL NOTE.

JOSEPH TUCKERMAN was born in Boston, Massachusetts, on the 18th of January, 1778. In 1798 he graduated from Harvard College, which in later years conferred the degree of Doctor of Divinity upon him. He then studied for his profession, and was settled over a parish in Chelsea in 1801, where he remained for twenty-five years. During this time he was instrumental in forming the "American Seaman's Friend Society," the first of its kind in the United States, for whose benefit he wrote a number of tracts which had large circulation.

In 1826 he removed to Boston, to begin "The Ministry at Large," a city mission for the poor on a broad basis, which soon came to be connected with "The Benevolent Fraternity of Churches," an association of several parishes for coöperative charity.

During a visit to Europe in 1833-4, he assisted in establishing the Ministry at Large in London and Liverpool, besides greatly stimulating work of a like nature in other places. In this work he continued to labor until 1838, when his health broke down completely. He died in Havana March 20th, 1840.

His life was one of self devotion and earnest labor for the good of others. His "Poor's Purse" was kindly supplied with voluntary subscriptions from those whose sympathy was excited by his stirring words and deep love of his work ; and notably by a Society of Ladies who called themselves "The Tuckerman Sewing Circle," and met monthly for the sale of their own works of ingenuity, passing the proceeds over to him. This Society still exists, and still continues its charitable labors. The impetus which he gave to intelligent philanthropy has not yet passed away, either in this country or in England.

The list of his printed works which is here appended is necessarily imperfect, as he kept no record of them. He contributed largely to the "Monthly Anthology and Boston Review," the "North American Review," the "Christian Examiner," and other periodicals ; and wrote many tracts for sailors and others, some of which went through a number of editions.

LIST OF PRINTED WORKS.

*** The publications of Mr. Tuckerman in the libraries named are indicated by letters as follows: H., Harvard University; B., Boston Athenæum; A., American Antiquarian Society.

1. A Funeral Oration occasioned by the death of General George Washington, before the Boston Mechanic Association. Boston, 1800. 8vo, pp. 24. H. B. A.

2. A Sermon before the Ancient and Honorable Artillery Company. Boston, 1804. 8vo, pp. 23. H. B. A.

3. Seven Discourses on Miscellaneous Subjects. Boston, 1813. 12mo, pp. 180. A.

4. A Sermon at the Ordination of Rev. Samuel Gilman. Charleston, S. C., 1820. 8vo, pp. 46. H. B. A.

5. Two Sermons preached at Marblehead. Salem, 1820. B.

6. A Sermon on the Twentieth Anniversary of his Ordination. Boston, 1821. 8vo. H. B. A.

7. A Discourse before the Society for propagating the Gospel among the Indians and others in North America. Cambridge, 1821. 8vo, pp. 48. B. A.

8. A Sermon at the Ordination of Rev. Orville Dewey. New Bedford, 1824. 8vo, pp. 41. H. B. A.

9. Letter on the principles of the Missionary Enterprise. Boston, 1826. 12mo. H. B.

10. Extract from an Address. 1826. 12mo.

11.   Quarterly Reports as Minister at Large, 1826, 1827. H. B.

12.   A Sermon: Religion a Practical Principle.   1828.   B.

13.   Semi-annual Reports, &c., 1828–1833.   H. B.

14.   A Letter to Hon. Harrison Gray Otis, respecting the House of Correction and Common Jail in Boston. 1830. 12mo.

15.   Prize Essay on the Wages paid to Females.   Philadelphia, 1830.   12mo.   H. B.

16.   Report of the Commissioners appointed by the Order of the House of Representatives on the Pauper System of the Commonwealth.   Boston, 1832.   8vo.   H.

17.   Report on a Farm-School.   1832.   8vo.

18.   Introduction to the American translation of Degerando's Visitor of the Poor.   1832.   12mo, pp. 30.   H. B.

19.   A Sermon: the Gospel a Blessing to the Poor.   1832.   B.

20.   A Letter to the Executive Committee of the Benevolent Fraternity of Churches, on the Ministry at Large.   1834.   8vo.   B.

21.   A Sermon at the Ordination of C. F. Barnard and F. T. Gray as Ministers at Large.   1834.   8vo.   H. B.

22.   Address on the Obligation of Christians to become Ministers.   Newcastle, England, 1834.

23.   The First Annual Report of the Association of Delegates from the Benevolent Societies of Boston.   1835.   12mo.   H. B.

24.   Gleams of Truth, or Scenes from Real Life.   1835.   H.

25.   A Letter respecting Santa Cruz as a Winter Residence, addressed to Dr. J. C. Warren.   1837.   8vo.   H.

26.   The Principles and Results of the Ministry at Large in Boston.   1838.   12mo, pp. 327.   H. A.

27.   Joseph Tuckerman on the Elevation of the Poor. A Selection from his Reports as Minister at Large in Boston. With an Introduction by Edward Everett Hale.   Boston, 1874. 12mo, pp. 206.   H. A.

A FUNERAL ORATION

OCCASIONED BY THE DEATH OF

General George Washington.

A FUNERAL ORATION

OCCASIONED BY THE DEATH OF

General George Washington.

WRITTEN AT THE REQUEST OF THE

Boston Mechanic Association,

AND

Delivered before them, on the 22d of FEB. 1800.

By JOSEPH TUCKERMAN.

Consulere patriæ, parcere afflictis fera
Cæde abstinere, tempus atque iræ dare,
Orbi quietem, sæculo pacem suo.
Hæc summa virtus; petitur hac cœlum via.

SENECA.

BOSTON:

PRINTED BY MANNING & LORING.

At a Meeting of the Trustees of the Mechanic Association, Feb. 22, 1800.

ON Motion, Voted, That the Thanks of the President and Trustees of this Association, in behalf of the Mechanic Interests of the Town of *Boston*, be presented to MR. JOSEPH TUCKERMAN, for the pathetic, elegant and judicious Oration, commemorative of the sublime virtues and pre-eminent Services of the late GENERAL WASHINGTON, delivered by him this Day; and that he be requested to furnish a Copy thereof for the Press.

A true Copy of Record, JAMES PHILLIPS, *Sec'ry.*

BOSTON, *February* 24, 1800.

SIR,

WE have the Pleasure to communicate the following unanimous Vote of the Board of Trustees of the Mechanic Association; and to assure you of the respectful Consideration with which we have the honor to be,

Your most obedient, humble Servants,

JONATHAN HUNNEWELL,
BENJAMIN RUSSELL,
WILLIAM TODD.

Mr. JOSEPH TUCKERMAN.

BOSTON, *February* 24, 1800.

GENTLEMEN,

WITHOUT apology, I present to you the Oration written at your request. Its favorable reception demands my gratitude; and I only desire, that it may be perused with that candor, which should ever distinguish those productions, which derive their principal merit from the subject by which they are occasioned.

I am, Gentlemen,

With great respect,

Your humble Servant,

JOSEPH TUCKERMAN.

Mr. JONATHAN HUNNEWELL,
Mr. BENJAMIN RUSSELL,
Mr. WILLIAM TODD.

WASHINGTON.

Mr. President, and
Gentlemen of the Mechanic Association,

WE have assembled to commemorate an event, which will ever be considered as one of the most interesting and melancholy, in the history of our country. An event, which, as it awakens every mournful sensation, should also excite our gratitude to him who is the disposer of all things, and to whose divine interpositions we are indebted for our freedom, sovereignty and independence.

IT is, Gentlemen, perfectly consistent with the character which you have uniformly presented, to meet at this time, in order to pay the last respects to the memory of your departed friend and political father. Many of your interest have shared with him, the arduous toils in which he was engaged, and by the firmness of their conduct, acquired those stations, which could be gained only by superior merit. With these advantages, you are sensible of his worth, and are desirous of exhibiting the only testimony of affection which is now in your power. To this exercise you are prompted by the best inclinations of your natures; and he who has implanted gratitude in man, and given him a spirit to understand and to support his rights, will look with an approving smile on this pleasing and instructive duty.

On this day, we have been accustomed to indulge the fervor of our love, in celebrating the birth of WASHINGTON. A recollection of the services which he performed, of the dangers to which he was exposed, and the unparalleled magnanimity which he at all times discovered, then

served to keep alive the flame of patriotism in our breasts, and constantly to render
his character more dear to our minds. On
this occasion, every heart exulted, and every
tongue proclaimed his praise. We reverted
to the season, when, governed by foreign
laws and foreign manners, we existed only
as the tributaries of a nation, to whose
command our resources were subjected,
and by whose authority every action was
controlled. The powerful contrast between
this condition and that which was secured
to us by the first of men, called forth the
warmest effusions of our souls, and induced
us to behold him as formed by Heaven,
for the accomplishment of this great and
important end. To him, we traced all the
happiness which resulted from liberty, and
all the blessings which were attached to a
free Constitution.

But for the testimonials of joy, we now
substitute the badges of grief; and the
pleasure which beamed from every countenance, is exchanged for the gloominess

of sorrow. If then it be permitted to regret the loss of a friend, endeared to us by a similarity of sentiment; if we may lament a removal of our benefactor, who has interfered in the hour of distress, and rescued us from ruin; if we may indulge our reflections on the deprivation of a parent, who has sacrificed his own to procure our enjoyment; or rather, who has found his highest satisfaction in promoting our felicity, it cannot be deemed improper to express our feelings, when death has taken from us one, in whom all these characteristics were connected. Let us then endeavor to analyze the life, and to display the merits of our illustrious Chief. These are so well known, that a relation of them, will only be a recurrence to those impressions, which are deeply engraven on the memories of all.

GENERAL WASHINGTON was born on the twenty-second of February, seventeen hundred and thirty-two, and was the son of a planter, residing in the State of Virginia. Under the direction of a private tutor, he imbibed those maxims, which have consummated his greatness, and secured for his country an unrivalled respect among the nations of the world. His desire for military attainments, presented itself among the first impulses of his mind. At the early age of fifteen, when youth, accustomed only to the domestic circle, shrinks from the appearance of danger, he had made preparations to enter the marine service in the capacity of a midshipman. Yielding however to the solicitations of a fond mother, he abandoned this favorite intention. Scarce four years had elapsed, before he was again invested with the insignia of a soldier; and such were the extent of his views, the richness of his invention and the fortitude of his mind, that at twenty-one he was deputed on a commission, which required for its execution the hardihood of a veteran, and the skill of an accomplished General. His remonstrances not being attended with the desired effect, he was sent to gain by his prowness, what the force of argument would not produce; and in his conquest at Redstone, he gave a prelude of those abilities, which, but a short time after this, saved from destruction the scattered forces of a British officer,* whose haughty spirit disdained to receive instruction from one, so much younger than himself in the arts of war.

At the establishment of peace in seventeen hundred and sixty-three, he retired to his estate, to cultivate the milder virtues of private life; and formed that connexion, from which he anticipated his future happiness. At this time he probably acquired that love of retirement, which appeared so conspicuous through the rest of his life. In seventeen hundred and seventy-four, he was a member of the Continental Congress; and on the fifteenth of June, '75, was unanimously chosen by them, commander in chief of the American armies. The manner in which he performed this duty, through the long and

* General Braddock.

tedious space of eight years will not require a recital. Or, if any would ask for evidences, we would point to almost every part of our extensive country. We would ask him to behold the present state of our nation, which, under GOD, is indebted to his exertions, for the greatest portion of the respectability by which it is distinguished.

AMONG the many instances of valor which appear in his life, we might advert to the prudent, yet determined conduct, which preserved this town from the destructive fury of its disappointed adversaries. We might call your attention to witness the immortal glory which he acquired at York, Trenton, Monmouth and Princeton. But it will be sufficient at this time to observe, that having to regulate, to clothe and to arm an undisciplined body of men ; and not only to contend with the power of his enemies, but with the doubts, the prejudices and the wants of those who had enlisted under his banners, he achieved those wonders, which will ever command the admiration of the world. He was, in effect, the absolute ruler of our nation; and from his acceptance of the supreme command, to his resignation in seventeen hundred and eighty-three, its whole operations were directed by his counsels.

Our rights being secured, the necessity of establishing them on a permanent foundation was soon perceived. The disordered state of our finances, and the derangement of our public affairs urged the immediate performance of this. And in the Convention assembled for the purpose, WASHINGTON was elected to the Presidential chair.

In seventeen hundred and eighty-nine, he was elevated by his countrymen to the dignity of President of the United States; and having twice officiated in this capacity, with that wisdom which was peculiar to himself, he again took his leave of public life. He descended from the most honorable station in which he could be placed by the power of man, to the humble rank of a citizen. I say the most honorable station, because it was given by the suffrages of a free people, who were acquainted with the excellence of his character, and the benefits, which from this source had resulted to his country. His farewell address contains the principles on which his government was founded; and comprises a system of national policy, unexampled in ancient or modern times. An observance of its directions will lead to true greatness, and furnish characters like himself, to perpetuate our glory and our happiness.

THE official letters of General WASHINGTON, during our revolutionary war, will be preserved as a record of the strength of his abilities, the purity of his motives, and the address with which he treated every subject connected with his station. They will teach your children the hardships which he encountered, the discouragements which appeared at every step of his progress, and the unshaken virtue which he exercised, even in situations, where it could scarcely be deemed a crime to deviate. In perusing these, they will contemplate with wonder, his soldiers unused to war, and wavering through fear at those periods when fortitude was most essential; and yet, with his assistance, performing works, which would have reflected honor on troops inured to toil, and accustomed to success. But they will particularly observe his reliance on the Providence of ALMIGHTY GOD, and the firmness of his mind, which proceeded from a consciousness that he was contending only for that freedom, which the GOD of nature intended for his rational offspring. Liberty, and not conquest, was the object of his wishes; and so plainly does this appear, that even calumny has not dared to offer a contradictory insinuation.

IF we were here to close our retrospect of the conduct of this wonderful man, posterity would consider no additions as necessary for the completion of his virtues. As a hero and legislator he will ever stand superior to competition, and be quoted as a model of all which can dignify the character, and secure glorious fame. But if we contemplate him in his retreat, interested indeed for the welfare of his country, yet unambitious of preferment; if we view him as acting in the capacity of a common juror; and again, when our privileges were endangered by foreign aggression, consenting to quit the scenes of tranquillity to which he had become strongly attached, and accepting a second situation in command, we shall acknowledge that he has attained the summit of human excellence, and that panegyric is lost in the mention of his name.

WASHINGTON in early life, possessed a warm and impetuous disposition. This was probably the cause, which incited him so early to commence that career, which has been so honorable to himself and so productive to his country. But with a heart which was influenced by every tender sensibility, he corrected that ardour, which might otherwise have produced the most unhappy effects. He knew how to mingle ambition with humility; zeal, with prudence; and a love of his country, with a love of mankind. He possessed the most essential qualities of the most renowned men; and has been so wise, yet unaffected in every measure which he proposed; so regular, yet resolved in every action, that in a review of his virtues, we know not which most to commend. By his unvaried presence of mind, he secured the admiration of the brave, and by his caution, he won their confidence; by the judiciousness of his administration, he acquired the esteem of that band of patriots over whom he presided; and by the purity of his life, gained the affection of the good, and the hallowed remembrance of ages yet unborn.

THE character of the beloved hero, whose death we deplore, was marked with those traits, which are rarely to be discerned among the conquerors of mankind. Christian benevolence glowed in his heart, and animated his conduct in every situation. To be generous, is ever the characteristic of a brave man. It is a quality so nearly related to true courage, that wherever it cannot be perceived, we pronounce the action to be rash and unmanly. Every imputation of this kind was avoided, by that spirit of humanity, which was mingled with every deliberation. He fought only for the religion and civil rights, which were bestowed on us by the GOD whom we served, and used no other methods for the acquisition of these, than what were consistent with the end which he proposed. In passing with him through the late contest, which terminated in the independence of our country, we may indeed lament, that so many fell as victims of delusion; but we must love the heart, which melted with pity for the sufferings of an adversary; we must venerate the man to whom no one was indifferent, and who possessed those feelings, which equally recommended him to friends and foes. The trade of war was to him unknown. And that systematical cruelty, which within a few years has desolated families, extirpated thousands from the earth, and immolated on its bloody shrine, the innocent mother, with her helpless children, was avoided by his mild and pacific temper, which was formed by a love of the religion of the Prince of Peace.

To benevolence so refined, he added that humility, without which, greatness loses half its charms. He was never actuated by that pride, which would elevate him above those to whom his services were devoted. But viewing himself as one, who, with the rest was to partake of the sweets, for which they were mutually laboring, he considered no man, however low, as undeserving of his notice. He possessed a dignity to which few could rise ; but in him, it was without any mixture of pride. It originated from the harmony of his mind, which gave order to all that he performed. A truly humble spirit is equally distant from that arrogance, which can contemplate only its own merit; and that meanness and pusillanimity, which dares not aspire to active virtue. In him it was an operating principle, which appeared in all his behavior; and gave to his character that mild but uniform lustre, which will continue brilliant, when those, who in idea have embraced the subjugation of the world, shall be sunk in darkness.

To a humble mind, he united an equanimity of temper, which enabled him to act with undeviating propriety. Amid the disorders of a tent, and the confusion of battle, his thoughts were composed, and his commands the result of meditation. The greatest warriors who have appeared, have stamped on their names an indelible disgrace, by submitting to those turbulent passions, which a trivial disappointment has occasioned. The biography of heroes, is generally a catalogue of crimes. They have legalized murder, to gratify some prevailing propensity. But in him, to whom we are now directing your view, there was displayed an uninterrupted regularity. He was calm in reflecting on every action, and unmoved in the hour of danger. And, if we remember the difficulties through which he passed, the obstacles he was obliged to surmount, and the unwearied patience which he preserved, we shall without hesitancy, place his morality, among the most distinguished which has adorned the nature of man,

Such were the virtues which appeared in his life; and they originated from that pure source, from whence alone real worth can flow. Of this we have an undeniable testimony, in the legacy which, with parental tenderness, he has bequeathed to us. Having there connected religion with morality, he has made them indispensable supports of political prosperity; and exhorted us not to indulge supposition, that one can be maintained without the other. Reason and experience join to convince us, that religion is the firmest cement of civil government ; and they who would oppose this, are not merely the enemies of one state, or nation, but of mankind. The ancient law-givers, to ensure the success of their systems, added to them the authority of the gods : And the modern philosophy, which has been substituted for the doctrines and precepts of the gospel, presents a melancholy instance of that depravity, to which those morals are always subject, which are not established by a sanction, higher than human resolution. Thus piety was a striking feature of his life. Without this, he might indeed have been a conqueror, and enrolled his name among the murderers of mankind. Without this, he might have attained fame and affluence. But his riches would then have been only new means of corruption, and his reputation serve but to extend the curses which would attend it. Instead of this, we behold him, equally an example of piety and patriotism. With a love of his country, which can be compared only to his love of goodness, he has reared a fabric, which will continue so long as America is a nation ; and even when it is decaying with age ; when it yields to the ravages of time, will command astonishment, as magnificence in ruins.

Few are capable of knowing the trials of exalted stations. There are many vices, which from our peculiar situations we are not able to commit ; but when invested with power, we have a cloak, under which they may be concealed from the sight of man. It is the greatest temptation which we have to withstand in the present life. A love of glory leads to excesses, which the ability of gratifying, too frequently affords a sufficient palliation for the greatest crimes. But in the whole progress, through which we trace the footsteps of him whom we would now commemorate, we can perceive no marks, which lead even to a suspicion of guilt. The malignity of envy has not been able to place a spot on his name. In him, we behold one, whom elevation could not bewilder, nor flattery deceive. Who received power, as intrusted

to him, for the advantage of those by whom
it was bestowed; and desired more their
peculiar welfare, than his own aggrandize-
ment. We deduce this from evidence the
most incontrovertible; it is from his conduct; and its truth is so strongly impressed
on our minds, that a relation of it, precludes
the necessity of proof.

WITH a character so ennobled, we have
been favored. We mention it, not to boast
of his superiority, but to excite our gratitude. Surely we cannot recur to the
blessings, which Providence through him
has granted, without feeling those lively
emotions, which favors so signalized should
demand. He was the pride of his friends,
the glory of his country, and the wonder of
the world. By his public virtues, he acquired the admiration both of Europe and
America, and the most celebrated men of
the age have sought the honor of presenting their respects to him.* By his domestic

*As an attestation of this, three evidences may be cited,
which are indeed among the most signalized. Dr. Franklin in

qualities, he secured the affections of a family, whose happiness was interwoven with his own. He had all which could attach man to existence. His fame had extended as far as civilization, and his name was cherished, wherever virtue was loved. Hail sainted shade! Thou now inhabitest a happier clime. We would view thee, as among the children of the blessed. We would congratulate thee on the possession of a crown, which will continue with undiminished brightness, when the laurels of the present life shall fade, and be no longer a testimony of distinction. Thy name shall ever live in the memory of a grateful country, and thine actions be celebrated

his will, bequeathed his gold-headed cane to General WASHINGTON, accompanied with the remark, "If it were a sceptre, he would deserve it." He likewise received a sword from the King of Prussia, bearing the motto, "From the oldest, to the greatest General in the world." And from the Earl of Buchan, "a Box, made of the oak that sheltered the great Sir William Wallace after the battle of Falkirk. This box was presented to the Earl, by the Goldsmiths' company at Edinburgh; but feeling his *unworthiness* to receive this magnificently significant present, obtained leave to make it over to the man in the world, to whom he thought it most justly due."

with increasing honors.   We bid thee farewell.

On this occasion, we would sympathize
with the unhappy widow, who peculiarly
experiences the severity of this divine
dispensation ; and with the most sincere
affection, would commend her to him, to
whose presence, we trust, the disembodied
spirit of her husband has now ascended.

To the officers and soldiers of our armies,
we would offer him as an example through
every part of his life. We would demonstrate from his actions, that religion is not
incompatible with valor ; and urge them
to cultivate his virtues, as they would
attain his greatness.

To all classes of men, we would recom-
mend an obedience to the principles which
he has presented, as the best method of
testifying their sorrow for his loss ; or
rather, to yield an observance to his in-
junctions, whom WASHINGTON rejoiced
to obey.   We have been deprived of one,

on whom our reliance was placed without reserve. Let us endeavor as far as possible to repair this loss, by reposing the same confidence in ADAMS, his illustrious successor.

IT is worthy of remark, that in seventeen hundred and seventy-six, WASHINGTON was intrusted with a dictatorial power. If ambition had been his favorite passion, he might now have satiated his appetite. It may likewise be remembered, that at the close of the war, when the armies were disbanded and unpaid, that anonymous and inflammatory papers were circulated, to persuade the soldiers to rise, and to acquire by force, that redress, which it was not in the power of Government to bestow. At this time also, he might have taken the reins of empire, and made himself the monarch of our nation. But he quelled the tumult by his eloquence, and allayed those disordered feelings, which were ready to burst on the country just rescued from oppression. The better to display his merits in this respect, we might contrast him with the late invader of Egypt. We might oppose that disposition, which preferred the good of others, to his own fame; to that temper which stimulates man to hesitate at no sacrifice for the accomplishment of his object, and to consider power as an excuse for every crime, which the aspiring mind may dictate.

ATTEND, then, Warriors, Statesmen, Citizens! and behold one worthy of your imitation. Equally to be admired in peace and war; equally able to command and to obey. Governed by those eternal principles, which proceeded from the source of truth, he had learned to conquer himself, before he attempted to subdue others. He whose military character will form a new epoch in the pages of history; whose wisdom in design, and prudence in action, will vie with the united sagacity of the most celebrated heroes, was a votary of religion. While therefore we indulge the language of grief; while with drooping hearts and dejected countenances, we pause at a remembrance of the loss we have sustained, let us raise our eyes to heaven ; and recurring to the blessings of which he is participating, anticipate the time when we may dwell with him forever.

FINIS.

SEVEN DISCOURSES

ON

MISCELLANEOUS SUBJECTS.

MISCELLANEOUS SUBJECTS.

———

BY J. TUCKERMAN, A. M.

———

BOSTON:

PUBLISHED BY MUNROE AND FRANCIS,

At the Shakspeare Bookstore, No. 4 Cornhill.

1813.

CONTENTS.

DISCOURSE I.

ISAIAH iii. 10.

*Say ye to the righteous, it shall be well with him, for
the reward of his hands shall be given him.*

IN what consists the chief good of man?
This is an inquiry which all should be able
readily to answer. It is an inquiry which
should early be proposed to every one, and
on which every parent should assist his
children to form the most correct sentiments, before their entrance into the world.
By the ideas which we form of the chief
good of life, not only our earliest tastes,
affections, and pursuits are biassed, but our
characters in this world are determined,
and our conditions in the future.

In what then consists the chief good of life? and what are the means of attaining it? We all agree, my brethren, in the general definition, that happiness is the best good of man. But what is happiness? This too is an inquiry, which every one should be able to answer; but I believe, on no subject are opinions more vague and indeterminate. Often, when we profess to be happy, we know not why we are so; and when we can give a reason for it, it is often surprising to all but ourselves, that such a cause should be productive of such an effect. But are those emotions of momentary pleasure, which may be repressed as easily as they were excited, which are as variable as our bodily sensations, and which may be made the sport of every passion, worthy of the name of happiness? Can these be the best good of man? Have the insatiable desires which every one experiences, no higher means of gratification? Are there no satisfactions, in their own nature more complete, more permanent? It does not require a laborious investigation of the faculties and capacities of man, to learn that it was the intention of our Creator that we should seek and possess a happiness, far more elevated and durable. What then is this happiness? Are we to seek it within, or without us? Does it belong to the mind, or to the body? We all consider health as an inestimable blessing; yet neither we, nor those about us, are happy in proportion to our health. Property too is a good which all are seeking, and for which all are solicitous. Yet it is certain, that wealth alone will not render us happy. It is obvious, that some of the most affluent are the most miserable of men. A vigorous understanding is desirable. But how often is it accompanied with appetites and passions, destructive of order and peace? We admire the works of a luxuriant and cultivated imagination, and some are ready to envy its possessor, supposing that *he* must surely be happy, who is capable of exciting such sensations in others. But fancy exerts its creative power, as frequently in producing wretchedness as pleasure. Shall we then seek for happiness in fame? This is indeed a good which all highly estimate. Sweet to every ear is the voice of praise, and most grateful to all would be the conviction, that their memories would be cherished, when they had themselves left the world. But will the applause of the world repress the passions, which impel to excesses, and prey upon the peace of the mind? Will they silence the reproaches of conscience, and inspire confidence in death?—Or may we hope to obtain it in the indulgence of the senses? The eye is not satisfied with seeing, nor the ear with hearing. And do you think that the epicure, the lascivious, the intemperate man is happy? Alas! show me one who, in either of these courses, has found that happiness which the rational, the immortal soul demands, and I will submit to his guidance; I will follow him in every step of his successful pursuit. But where is he? I know him not. But who does not know, that each of these paths has conducted

thousands to disease, to unutterable anguish, and to premature death? Must all
our inquiries then be vain? Is happiness
but a phantom, which mocks alike our
solicitations and our labours? Are we
mistaken in the sentiment which we have
so fondly cherished, that there is a good,
in the possession of which the mind does
not anxiously crave anything beyond it?
No, my friends. God does not thus sport
with his creatures. The insects, the birds,
the beasts, apparently at least, enjoy all of
which they are capable. Why then are
the enjoyments of man so far below the
standard of his capacities? The reason is
plain. We seek happiness in objects which
were not designed to confer it. We attach
our strongest affections to pursuits and
gratifications, which involve disappointment and wretchedness. Where then is
the seat of happiness? I answer, in the
heart. And what are the means of attaining it? I reply, a life of obedience to the
will of God. Every act of virtue, performed from a principle of obedience to

the will of God, is a means of happiness. This principle is indeed the very soul of virtue, which is subject to none of the changes of the world, and is a perennial source of the purest pleasure. This is the truth, my brethren, which I would illustrate; and in what subject can any feel a deeper interest? All *would be* happy. All *may be* happy, who will live devoted to the will of God.

The object of this discourse is to shew, 1., that virtue is the best good of this life, because it secures the greatest happiness; and 2dly, if it did not secure the greatest happiness of this life, it would be infinitely the best good of man, because it involves the greatest, the eternal happiness of the future. "Say ye to the righteous, it shall be well with him; for the reward of his hands shall be given him."

1. Virtue is the best good of man, because it secures in this world his greatest happiness. By virtue I do not mean that limited and partial principle, which embraces only a few of our personal and

social duties. "An action, to be really virtuous, must flow from an internal principle, which is adapted to produce an *uniform* and a *regular* good conduct." This principle is *the love of God*, that first and great commandment of the gospel. "It is religion alone which, by uniting duty and happiness, can forever bind self-love to the interest of virtue." There is no true virtue distinct from religion, and there is no religion distinct from virtue. In the love of God alone, originates the proper love of ourselves, and that love of one another which is the end, or completion of the commandment. With these sentiments of virtue, I will endeavour to demonstrate by its present effects, that it is the best good which can be sought in this world.

In the first place then I observe, that virtue points us to an object, infinitely worthy of our best affections and efforts; to the pursuit of which we are guided by unerring principles, and in which we are certain that success will be the reward of perseverance. This object is the favour of God; the approbation of Him, whose power can satisfy our most extensive desires, and whose goodness, like his power, is infinite.

What can be of equal worth with the approbation of God; the favour of the Creator and Governour of the world; the greatest and the best of Beings? We value the esteem of men. It gives us a rank in society which we desire; it gratifies our self-love. But the consciousness of the approbation of God elevates us infinitely above the most exalted condition of this life. It awakens the ineffable satisfaction of feeling, that we are spiritually his children. In loving God supremely, our affections are exposed to no fluctuations, for his character in unchangeable; they are exposed to no disappointment, for he cannot deceive us. Every action to which we are prompted by the love of God, is a part of that service which he requires; and our duties, as individuals, as social beings, as dependents on the providence, and subjects of the government of God, are so plain, and so admirably adapted to every exigence of life, that an ingenuous mind cannot mistake them, nor will any thing be left for him to regret, by whom they are practised. In every other pursuit, we are liable to be mortified by unsuccessful endeavours, though all our skill be exerted to prevent it; but God beholds with favour *even a desire*, if it be *sincere*, of conforming to his will. He admits him who feels this desire to all the happiness and all the benefits of the most intimate intercourse, as a means of cherishing and strengthening it, and of securing its accomplishment. In this single view of its influence, is not virtue then conducive to the best happiness of this life? To be loved by God; to be assured that he hears our prayers; that all the events of his government are ordered by infinite wisdom and goodness, and that every action, performed with a design of pleasing him, is observed and accepted;— these surely are compensations for affliction, which should repress every doubt, and silence every murmur; they are sources of gratification pure and inexhaustible. The approbation of those whom we reverence and love is alone a reward of every privation and toil. It makes us rich in poverty; and is as a shield to our peace against all the slanders of the wicked. If virtue, then, obtained for us no other good than *the approbation of God*, the certainty that he beholds us with affection, it would be our best possession, because it renders us most independent of the world; independent even of the good opinion of the virtuous, who may misinterpret our best motives, and join with the vicious in condemning our best intended actions. It is a perfect security, that, whatever occurs, is precisely what we should ourselves have chosen, could we have discerned all the purposes of God. Can any happiness be more rational, more stable, more desirable?

2dly. Virtue secures our greatest happiness, by repressing the appetites and passions which occasion misery. Avarice, envy, jealousy, resentment, pride, vanity, intemperance and lust, are tyrants which corrupt the affections of the wicked, pervert their understandings, and enslave their wills. This is the language of the New Testament. "Whosoever committeth sin," says the Saviour, "is the servant of sin;" and "to whom ye yield yourselves servants to obey," says the apostle, "his servants ye are whom ye obey." Hence, said Jesus at the commencement of his ministry, "I am come to set at liberty them that are bound;" and, again, "if the son shall make you free, ye shall be free indeed." Is liberty a blessing? Behold in it, then, my brethren, one of the rewards of virtue. By the practice of virtue we are emancipated from the most ignoble bondage; from a bondage, compared with which, the most cruel slavery of the body is an inconsiderable evil. In the subjection of these despotick appetites and passions, consists the first triumph of virtue; and their conquest represses a thousand wants, and preserves us from the anguish of ten thousand sorrows.

Is it objected, that the subjugation of these appetites and passions is at best but a deliverance from many troubles, and not a means of certain happiness? Look at that avaricious being, who loves not even his soul so much as his wealth; who is at the same time tormented with desire to augment his useless stores, and agonized with fears, lest the inconstant elements, or the perfidy of man, should strip him of what he possesses. Would not a mere exemption from these sufferings be purchased cheaply, at the expence of all his wealth? Behold that man, whose mind and heart are corroded with envy! The superior wisdom of another, or his greater fortunes or influence, or even his more elevated virtues, make him an object of hatred. The envious man cannot think of his rival, without feeling at the same time the influence of every malignant desire; he cannot hear him praised, without unutterable suffering. Will you then call exemption from the power of this passion an inconsiderable good? Is not the man advanced far towards happiness, who is relieved from so much misery?—See that man whose soul is harassed with suspicions! He dashes from his lips the cup which is presented by the hand of friendship, which might quiet his agitations, and warm his heart with benevolence, and seizes with eagerness, and drinks to the very dregs, the draught which will extend the most subtle poison to every portion of his frame.—Behold the slave of revenge! To gratify his insatiate passion, how many miseries will he sustain; to how many dangers will he expose himself? Nor is he for a moment certain, that some new work is not preparing for him, by the inflexible tyrant whom he serves.—See the proud man, daily fretted with innumerable disappointments; alternately contemning and hating those about him, and in his turn, hated and despised by those, on whom he is necessarily dependent; a prey to cares which he cannot repress, and impelled to excesses, the destructive influence of which no exertions can repair.

—Behold the vain man, like the gaudy insect, glittering for a moment in the sun, and then by a breath of wind stripped of his wings, creeping unnoticed, or despised upon the ground.—Behold the slave of intemperance! Till he receives the portion which enfeebles and deranges his powers, and deadens his sensibility, he is wretched; and having recovered from its influence, he is the sport of every debasing passion, till he is again insensible.—See the poor abandoned servant of impure lusts! His pleasures are momentary; but not so are his pains. Disease infects his body, and remorse, with its sharpest stings, pierces his mind.—Yet each of these unhappy beings blindly follows the impulse of the passion or appetite to which he has surrendered himself. Hence, my brethren, far the greatest portion of the murmurs which assail our ears; far the greatest part of that debasement and distress, which we daily see in our intercourse with the world. In reducing these passions to obedience to its dictates, from how much misery does virtue defend us? But for the influence of these appetites and passions, how many do we know, who might daily enjoy all which the world could give them? It is the office of virtue to scourge these tyrants into subjection; and it is one of the distinguishing privileges of a good man, that he is delivered from their dominion. Does not virtue then promote the happiness of this life, far more than it could be advanced, even by the attainment of all the objects, to which these appetites and passions impel us? The happiness of virtue, compared with that of vice, is the happiness of freedom compared with that of slavery; it is the happiness of independence, compared with that of want. This is the second illustration of our text. "Say ye to the righteous, it shall be well with him." No evil propensity shall prey upon his peace. He shall be free to follow the guidance of the virtue which he loves; and in conforming to its dictates, he shall receive his reward.

3. Virtue secures an approving conscience. In the conviction of the approbation of God, and in the possession of
well balanced passions and well governed
appetites, what has man to want or to fear?
The happiness which a rational and accountable being should pursue, and which
alone is worthy of his exalted nature,
is the happiness of feeling that he has
accomplished, or is pursuing the object,
for which he received his existence and
faculties; that he has faithfully discharged
the duties, which grow out of his condition
and his various relations. Such a man
recurs to the past without remorse, and
looks to the future without apprehension.
His happiness is a column, resting on the
word of God; and which every action of
piety and virtue which he has performed,
has at once augmented and strengthened.
—The spirit of a good man may support
his infirmities. Under all the trials of
human life, he has a refuge within his own
breast, to which no assailants from without
can penetrate. In that self-approbation

which is sanctioned by the word of God, he can securely and tranquilly hear the storm which rages around him, satisfied that, while the world is governed by a being of infinite justice and goodness, not his safety only, but his peace is certain. But a wounded spirit; a condemning conscience; a mind aware of its guilt, too irresolute to reform, and anticipating the threatened judgments of the Almighty; a conscience tortured with remembrance, and dreading reflection, who can bear? Who, for the miserable gratifications of vice, would deliberately consent to endure this accumulation of horrors? Who, in the calm moment of serious consideration, would not forego every other possession and pleasure, for a conscience void of offence toward God and man? This, likewise, my friends, is the rich reward of virtue. It is a happiness which belongs only to the virtuous. "The wicked is like the troubled sea, when it cannot rest, whose waters throw up mire and dirt." "There is no peace to the wicked, saith my God."

4thly. Virtue is also favourable to the acquisition of riches. Do not think, my brethren, that I wish to support the absurd sentiment, that the virtuous are always successful in the pursuit of the interests of this world; and that, because a man is rich, he is therefore virtuous. No. Thousands of the best disciples of Christ, like their master, are poor. But it is a general truth, that success is the reward of uprightness; and though many prosper by knavery, that the dishonest and cunning are ensnared by their own projects, and are often ruined by the means which they have devised for the destruction of others. In the virtuous we may repose implicit confidence; and when they are known, they receive the patronage and support of the upright. And to an honest man, how valuable are his gains! He has obtained no part of them by the sacrifice of a principle. No one accuses him in the court of his own conscience; no one can accuse him at the throne of God. If he be rich then, riches are to him means of happiness, for they are means of doing good. But, my brethren, should a good man be unfortunate, he has the high consolation of reflecting that his misfortunes were not occasioned by his crimes. If he be poor, he has *only* the burden of *poverty* to sustain, which is light as the dust of the balance, when compared with the oppressive, the intolerable weight of a guilty conscience. If virtue does not confer wealth, it bestows that which is of infinitely greater worth, the ability and disposition cheerfully to sustain the privations of poverty; and he who has maintained his integrity, though he have lost all beside, has a treasure, which he who knows its worth, would not barter for the world. Will you then, for any of the gifts of fortune, exchange this happiness? Be not deceived. I have seen the wicked in great prosperity, and spreading himself like a green bay tree; but he passed away, and lo he was not; I sought him, but he could not be found. But mark the perfect man, and behold the upright! whether he be rich, or whether he be poor, he is blessed. His wants are conformed to his circumstances. No turbulent and craving passions disturb his repose, and restrain him from the discharge of duties. In his pursuits, whatever they are, he is cheerful; and his gains, however small, are enjoyed with gratitude. Do you desire this happiness? Be virtuous.

5. "A good name," says the wise man, "is better than precious ointment;" but the consciousness of deserving it is still better than its possession. We naturally desire the esteem of those about us; but a permanent respect and affection can be obtained only by virtue, which generally commands deference, even from the abandoned. Virtue, indeed, does not always insure an unsullied reputation. It is the mark at which the vicious most delight to direct the arrows of slander. But what is the reputation which will render us happy? Not the noisy applause of an ignorant multitude. Not the flattery of those who are interested to praise us. But the estimation of good men. The approbation

which is induced by a knowledge of our principles, motives, and conduct. Other esteem than this a good man would reject as unworthy of him, and this a good man alone possesses. He is honoured by those whom he honours; who love virtue, and who practise it. This is a source of rational pleasure. It is alone a compensation for all the calumnies of the world. But suppose a man of real virtue to become an object of general jealousy and detraction. Think you that the loss, even of the esteem of the wise and good, is the loss of happiness? No. The virtue which deserves commendation, is an adequate support under every pressure of obloquy. He knows that the cloud which envelops him will soon be dissipated; and like the sun, which, after the obscurity of a few days, is hailed with redoubled gladness, his darkened reputation will emerge with apparently increased brightness, and among the virtuous, will diffuse increased joy and confidence. It is the happiness of a good man, that he fears not to be known. He

8

has worn no disguise. He has practised no artifices. He dreads no scrutiny. Is not reputation, thus obtained, thus supported, conducive to happiness? I pity the man who views it with indifference. He must be as dead to real happiness, as he is to virtue.

6. One of the most delightful objects of the anticipation of the young is the interchange of affection in domestick life. To the conjugal and parental relations, to a home which we may peculiarly call our own, all look forward with sanguine expectations. But are these relations always productive of happiness? Are there no murmurs of discontent, no exclamations of vehement passion, which ever strike the ear in these retreats from the cares and troubles of the world? Alas! Ascend a rising ground, and look upon the dwellings which it exhibits. But even this effort is not necessary to discover the habitations of men, where the sweet influence of affection and peace is unknown. But whence all this discord, turbulence, and misery?

Whence this mortifying and distressing disappointment of the most sanguine and happy expectations? Is it not the natural and necessary influence of vice? Is it not the effect of vitiated appetites and ungoverned passions? It is not necessary then; it is not unavoidable. To be happy in our domestick relations, we have but to be virtuous. Let these passions be repressed, let these appetites be subdued, let the personal, social, and pious duties be faithfully performed, and every reasonable anticipation will be realized. A husband and wife united by the pure affections which christianity inculcates, rearing their children in the love of God and the practice of virtue, often enjoy all of which man is capable in this world; and in every affliction have a solace, which divests it of more than half its poignancy. The serenity of mind with which virtue inspires a good man, the gratitude, the benevolence, the forbearance, the integrity, the resignation which mark his conversation and conduct, extend their efficacy to all about him.

Whatever be his condition, in his home he is happy; and what trials, what sufferings may not be cheerfully sustained in our commerce with the world, while virtue receives its encouragement and reward, in the improvement, the warm affections, and the uncorrupted happiness of those who are most interested in us, and whom we most tenderly love?

7. I will suggest to you, my brethren, but one more proof, that virtue is the best good of this life, because it secures the greatest happiness;—It prepares us for death. It prepares us not only to meet dissolution, but to anticipate it with composure, and with hope. This is a general truth. That there are exceptions, that many of the most pious look to the end of life with most distressful apprehensions, is readily admitted. Nor have I reserved this argument to the last, because it is the most important. The future condition of man is to be determined, not by the manner in which he dies, but by the manner in which he lives. But there are seasons

in the life of every man, when the thought of death obtrudes itself too forcibly to be resisted ; and to be able to retain and to cherish it, with a conviction that it will bring us to judgment, and to eternity, it is necessary to elevate and to strengthen the mind and heart, by an habitual application of the principles of virtue. This and this only will enable us to view its approaches, and to anticipate its consequences, with humble confidence. There is indeed no virtue so entire in this world, as to be wholly unmixed with evil ; and no one who can claim any thing of God. But even to the imperfect virtue of those who seek their happiness in his service, are all the promises of the gospel addressed ; and under every change of condition may the good look to death, not only for exemption from suffering, but with the conviction that they must be happy, in the disposal of a Being of infinite and eternal holiness. From how many hours of anguish does this conviction and the hopes which it awakens, preserve them ? They may view every season of sickness as perhaps the last stage of a journey, which will bring them to the home which they love; to the friends who have gone before them; to innumerable holy spirits; to the Saviour; to God. Is not virtue then, in all its consequences, supremely lovely and desirable? It guards us from unnumbered ills. It enables us cheerfully to support all from which it does not defend us. It represses even the fear of death. These, my brethren, are some of our motives to its practice.

But let us, for a moment, suppose that virtue, or religion did not secure to us the happiness of this life; that there was uniformly in this world, one event to him that served God, and to him that served him not;—let us suppose, that virtue was even more depressed and afflicted than vice, and that, in proportion to our moral and religious attainments, our sufferings were continually augmented. Still would virtue be infinitely our greatest good; the object deserving of all our affections and labours; an adequate compensation for every trial and distress in which it might involve us; for virtue is immortal; it will be followed by eternal happiness in the life which awaits us. Here then is an inexhaustible source of motives to its exercise. The moment of death, to a good man, is the commencement of eternal and of unalloyed enjoyment. Death forever terminates his cares, his pains, his toils, his sorrows. The happiness of the wicked, however great, lasts no longer than their life in this world. To them, death is the commencement of unutterable wo. But in the eternity which awaits the good, no interruption of their joys will be known. And what is eternity? What is eternal happiness?—Add millions to millions, till all the powers of your mind are exhausted by calculations; and you are still at an infinite distance. Suppose this earth, and all the mighty systems of worlds were brought into one mass; and from this pile of inconceivable greatness, one little particle of sand only should be taken in the revolution of hundreds of millions of years. What would be the term of time required for the removal of the whole? What in comparison with eternity? An instant. Nothing. Eternity still remains unchanged; and the happiness of the good unabated. Are such the rewards of virtue? O my God! who then can be vicious?

In persuading you then to a religious life, we consult, my friends, your highest interests, your greatest happiness. To be virtuous, is to walk in all the commands and ordinances of the Lord blameless; and these are the excitements by which the Spirit of God is striving with us, to maintain a life unspotted by the world. O be not inconsiderate, I pray you, of motives so powerful. In the pursuits of virtue, even in this world, you will have peace; a peace surpassing the imagination of the wicked; and they will conduct you to interminable bliss. When you know the will of God, delay not then to perform it. His will is the foundation of virtue, and his eternal favour its reward. Receive *Him* then, my brethren, with all gratitude, who is the way, the truth, and the life ; the only saviour of sinners. Study his gospel with devotion and diligence, and seek, through him, the illumination and guidance of the spirit of God. Then will it be well with you. Well in your consciences, and well in your families. Well in all the commerce of the world ; well in all your misfortunes and sufferings ; well in death ; and well in eternity.

9

DISCOURSE II.

JOHN viii. 34.

Whosoever committeth sin, is the servant of sin.

THIS truth is simple and obvious. The ancient philosophers taught their disciples, that a man was the slave of the lust which he obeyed. It is a truth which is recognized by us in our daily conversations; and if it obtained the influence which it demands, its effects would be most important on our virtue and happiness. But we acknowledge the bondage of sin, and we submit to it. We do more. We deliberately load ourselves with its chains. There are even some who devote the best energies of their minds and bodies, to the security of their own condemnation.

There is not indeed, my brethren, a just man upon earth, who doeth good and sinneth not. But though the most virtuous may, and do sin, they indulge in no *habitual* transgression of the law of God. By the remembrance of their offences they are penetrated with shame, and impelled to the throne of God to sue for pardon, and the grace which they need to guide, to guard and to comfort them. The terms righteous and unjust, good and wicked, saint and sinner, are relative. He is righteous, he is good, he is recognized as a saint in the gospel, who habitually acknowledges God, and endeavours to conform his temper and life to the divine will; who struggles against his vicious propensities, and seeks the assistance of the word and spirit of God to subdue them; who exercises and cherishes his benevolent and pious affections, who is deeply humble and penitent for his offences, and who

lives with a daily reference to his account-
ability, and his eternal destiny. He is
unjust, he is wicked, he is a sinner, who
lives without God; who violates his laws
without repentance; who seeks his happiness in the indulgence of passions, of
affections, and of appetites, which the
divine laws require him to deny; on whom
the means of religion are inefficacious, and
who is inconsiderate of the account which
he must render, and the sentence which
awaits him. Vice indeed has its degrees,
as well as virtue; and it may be as difficult
to name a man so depraved, that he has
not one sentiment or affection which we
could approve, as one who has never
transgressed any law, nor omitted any
duty. But very different, in the sight of
God, is a man of this imperfect, but sincere
piety and virtue, from him who cherishes
passions and indulges habits, which he
knows are forbidden in the gospel, and to
which are attached its solemn denunciations; who repeats iniquitous practices
without remorse, or if remorse be excited,

represses it, by plunging more deeply into evil indulgences; who sacrifices to vicious gratifications, not only the best pleasures of this life, but all the hopes and the fears of the future. This habitual sinner is in the most debased condition of man. It is to him that the Saviour refers when he says, *whosoever committeth sin, is the servant of sin.* He is not less submissive to his corrupt propensities, than is the most abject slave to the most despotick of masters.

1. Sin *enslaves* the understanding. "The understanding is the faculty of the soul, by which we assent to propositions, or dissent from them."* Truth and falsehood, vice and virtue, order and confusion, are not arbitrary terms; but are as distinct as light from darkness, and the distinction is as clearly discerned by an unvitiated mind. But this distinction is not obvious to a sinner; for by his love and practice of vice, his understanding either becomes too enervated for exertion, or so perverted as

* Hartley on man, vol. I, p. 3.

to blend the most contradictory principles. Is not he, then, that committeth sin, the servant of sin?

It is an immediate tendency of some vices, so to *enervate* the understanding, as to indispose or disqualify it for the exertions which are requisite, to distinguish truth from falsehood, and vice from virtue. Of this number is intemperance. There are men, who feel anxiety for no higher object, than what they shall eat or what they shall drink; whose thoughts and affections are as completely absorbed in the gratification of these appetites, as if this was the highest object of their being. For this they labour. For this they value their possessions; to this they devote their time, and by it are their hopes and their fears most powerfully excited. Can any dominion be more entire? But a small portion of time is indeed given to the actual indulgence of these appetites. They are satiated in a few moments; but the effects which they produce are not momentary nor inconsiderable. The very

delight with which this indulgence is anticipated, debases the noblest powers of the
mind; and in a moment it reduces the
most vigorous understanding, to worse
than infantile weakness. The epicure rises
from his luxurious repast, and the glutton
returns from his excesses, not to engage
in pursuits which demand a vigorous in-
tellect, but either to relieve the wearied
system by sleep, or to dissipate by some
amusement the dull and heavy hours which
must intervene, before the cloyed appetites will again demand their accustomed
gratification. The drunkard daily suffers
a temporary derangement. From the moment in which he receives the intoxicating
draught, till the relaxed frame regains its
vigour by repose, the authority of reason
is lost; and when he awakes from a sleep,
in which he has been as insensible as the
bed or the earth on which he lay, or dis-
turbed by a thousand horrid images, exhibited to his bewildered imagination, how
can he apply his mind to the labour of
thought? The severe exercises of the

understanding, for which they are always prepared, whose appetites are subjected to the dominion of reason and religion, to the intemperate, become at first so laborious, that in the fatigue which they occasion, an excuse is found for omitting them; and being for a short time neglected, this noble faculty is roused within them with scarcely less difficulty, than their bodies are excited to activity, when debilitated and diseased by the excesses to which they have been habituated. The instances are rare, and blessed be God that they are not more numerous, in which the power of reason is completely destroyed by the tyranny of the appetites; but who is ignorant of examples of their influence in enfeebling the understanding, and indisposing, or even disqualifying it, correctly to distinguish truth from errour, and vice from virtue? Who has not felt on his own reason, at some period of his life, the enfeebling influence of animal indulgence? Is not then the understanding of the epicure, the glutton, and the drunkard, enslaved by the lusts which they obey? The very excuses by which they palliate their guilt, evince the degraded state of that faculty, which, if freed from the restraints which they have imposed on it, would instantly convince them of their errour, their crime, and their misery. They cannot reason, or they reason, only as slaves serve the master whose will they dare not disobey. They attach their thoughts to few objects, which have not the most intimate connexion with their favourite gratifications. Thus is the understanding of him that committeth sin, the servant of sin. Thus are verified the words of the apostle, "of whom or of whatsoever a man is overcome, of the same he is brought in bondage."

Not less debilitating and debasing to the intellectual powers, are the pleasures of the epicure, the glutton, and the drunkard, than the gross and impure indulgences of the lascivious. Their minds partake of the relaxedness and pollution of their bodies. The excuses which they would once have alleged only to palliate their guilt, are soon adduced as arguments to justify the gratification of their bestial lusts; and they persuade themselves that they violate no law either of nature or reason, while every faculty of the mind is immersed in sensuality, and they degrade their immortal natures to a level with those of beasts which perish. Do not such examples forcibly illustrate the principle in our text, "He that committeth sin is the servant of sin?" Is not that man in the most miserable state of slavery, whose mind, enfeebled by sensual indulgence, sees no loveliness in virtue, and no pollution in impurity; who lives only to gratify the most ignoble desires of his nature; whose only standard of right and wrong is the immediate pleasure or pain of which an action will be productive, and who to his lusts sacrifices all those noble capacities, which would qualify him for a state of perfect intelligence and holiness?

As by some vices, the understanding is too debilitated to judge correctly, by others it is equally *perverted.* Foremost in the list of these vices are pride, worldly ambition, avarice, envy, jealousy, and resentment. These evil passions are not inconsistent with a vigorous exercise of the mind. They actuate many, whose understandings qualify them for the pursuit of the sublimest truth and the promotion of the most useful knowledge. But approach them nearly, and observe them in the exercise of their intellectual powers, and you will be convinced that these powers are enslaved; you will have new proof, that whosoever committeth sin, is the servant of sin; that by whom or by whatsoever the faculties of the mind are overcome, of the same they are brought in bondage.

Pride is a fashionable vice. It is dignified with the epithets of *honourable* and *laudable*. But what is pride? It is self-complacency, derived from a consciousness of being superiour to other men. It is a passion, which awakens equal contempt of others, as it produces of satisfaction with ourselves; and to retain its influence, it either conceals the excellencies of others beneath an impenetrable shade, or distorts them, or so magnifies its own, as to render all others undeserving of notice. Can a man in the full possession of the powers of his mind, thus reason and thus be happy? View the proud man. Lull his predominant passion to sleep, and engage him in a subject or a pursuit in which this passion is not interested, and you may find his perceptions clear, and his language and sentiments correct. But see him again when his pride is excited. He will oppose the most obvious truths, because they are suggested by one whom he deems an inferiour. He confounds humility with meanness, and has no conception that one can exist without the other. Meekness and forbearance are in his view evidences of a want of spirit; and the resentment of wrongs, if not a virtue, is at the worst, an errour of noble souls. He estimates opinions and characters, not by the unerring standard of truth, but by the contracted scale of his own prejudices; and admires or condemns, as his prevailing humour is gratified or disappointed. Is not the understanding of such a man enslaved by his pride? You may say that the powers of his mind are great, but if they act only in subserviency to this passion, is not his mind a servant of the lust which he obeys? —View the man also, in whom worldly ambition has obtained ascendancy. He thinks, he dreams of nothing, but of illustrious achievements or of loud applauses. He would live; how? In the breath of the multitude.—He would obtain; what? —honours which will wither, perhaps sooner than the first flowers which bloom upon his grave. To gratify this ambition, he sacrifices time, health and virtue; and he deems the offering small, if he can effectuate his purpose. Nay, not only would he sacrifice his own, but the lives, the fortunes, the reputations and the virtue, of thousands. Will the unvitiated reason of a man approve of this as the ultimate object of pursuit? Above all, will it approve of these means of accomplishing any object? Say then, if you please, that ambition is a splendid vice, but say not that the understanding of the ambitious man is free. His chains may dazzle your sight, and their glare may even render them imperceptible to himself; but the faculties of his mind are not on that account less enslaved. His understanding, if at liberty to examine and to judge, would denounce his favourite passion, and the means of indulging it, not less severely than they are denounced in the gospel.— Nor is the understanding of the avaricious man more free, than that of the ambitious and the proud. He attaches a supreme value to wealth, from which he anticipates no higher good, than the pleasure of beholding it. Is this a reasonable gratification? You acknowledge that the worth of riches, to a miser, is only imaginary; that his pains and his pleasures, though apparently excited by his successes and his misfortunes, do in fact result from the state of his own mind. Yet what is this but a concession, that his understanding is enslaved by his affection for the useless wealth which he has amassed? His soul is bound to his coffers, and scarcely does one thought escape the golden barriers which surround it. Give freedom to his understanding, and would he deem himself more rich, by the possession of millions which he never intends to use, than he is by a knowledge, that within the body of the earth are contained innumerable jewels of inestimable value?—Observe the envious, and say, if their understandings are not likewise enslaved by their prevailing passion? The liberty of reflection would soon cure this dreadful malady of the soul; but while envy is indulged, every thought, every desire, is attached to those possessions of another, which it would appropriate to itself. The envious man is not permitted to enumerate and to estimate his own blessings? or if this indulgence be allowed, it is only on condition, that he compares himself with those about him. Is not this a most debasing subjection of the mind? Is not he who thus committeth sin, a servant of sin?

—View the man also, whose jealous spirit is always awake, to catch every expression, and to notice every action, of the object by which it is excited. Can he reason calmly on the causes of his suspicion? Can he weigh evidence, and determine with impartiality? On other subjects, he may indeed be able to deliberate, and to give to every consideration the importance which it demands; but in the object of his jealousy, he can see nothing to justify, nor even to excuse. Every effort to please, he considers as an artifice to deceive him; and every virtue, which attracts the admiration and the love of others, in his apprehension, is but a gilded crime. Is not his understanding enslaved then by the passion which he obeys?—Observe likewise the man whose resentment is inflamed. He knows that he has committed a thousand offences against others, as great as that, which he is determined to revenge. He will acknowledge to you, in a dispassionate moment, that he has so often broken the laws of God, that without the divine mercy is extended to him, he has no hope of future happiness. Yet this man, who has so often experienced the clemency of others; this man, whose very existence is to be attributed to the forbearance of God; this man, who depends on sovereign and unmerited grace for future pardon and acceptance, cannot patiently submit to an expression or action, by which his expectations are disappointed. If he acquire for a moment a control of his thoughts, he is rendered humble, and penitent, and forgiving; but do not these very effects of reflection, demonstrate that the mind is enslaved, while it is influenced by resentful passions? Dreadful is the tyranny of revenge. Every faculty has been strained to its utmost point of exertion, to gratify its exorbitant demands. Every pursuit, every pleasure has been abandoned, that no thought and no care might interfere, with the accomplishment of its malignant designs. How forcible then, are the words of the apostle, "to whom we yield ourselves servants to obey, his servants we are whom we obey." How just and how full of instruction are the words of our Lord, he who committeth sin, is the servant of sin.

2. Sin enslaves the affections. "The affections have pleasure and pain for their objects, and by them we are excited to pursue happiness and to avoid misery, and all its apparent causes." In themselves they are innocent. It is only when attached to evil, that they become causes of guilt and wretchedness. "They are the winds, which, though often tempestuous, are necessary to convey the vessel to its port." If subject to the control of reason and religion, they will bear us smoothly and safely along, equally distant from the whirlpools of temptation, and the rocks and surges of disappointed expectation. But if the dominion of reason and religion be resigned, terrible will be the sufferings in which they will involve us. No gratification will be sought, but either of sense or passion; and every meanness and crime will be perpetrated, almost with-

out shame and remorse.—But let us con-
fine ourselves to the metaphor which is
used by our Lord. Sin enslaves the affections. To excite our love of piety and
virtue, and our abhorrence of iniquity,
God has attached to his laws, the most
glorious promises and the most awful
denunciations; he has made reputation,
health, and pleasure, the attendants of
virtue, and anguish and disease and disgrace the consequences of vice; he has
implanted within us the principle of conscience, to impel us to duty, and to restrain
us from transgression. But the practice
of evil being for a short time indulged, all
these restraints and motives yield to its
influence; and so strong does the love of
vice become, that men daily and deliberately commit it, even with pain, and disgrace, and death, and damnation in their
view. Does not sin enslave the affections
of the epicure, the drunkard, and the de-
bauchee? They supremely love the objects
to which these guilty passions are attached;
and sacrifice to them all which is most

interesting and dear in time and in eternity. Would a rational being, whose affections were free, attach them to objects, which necessarily produce ultimate ruin and misery? Is not this attachment, so abhorrent to reason, to duty, and happiness, a demonstration, that the affections of a sinner are in the most debased condition to which slavery can reduce them? Our affections are then free, when the happiness which they seek, or the misery which they avoid, is approved by conscience and the divine word; when we pursue and find pleasure in the path of duty. Then are there no jarring interests within us; no conflicts of discordant desires. However strong be our attachments, we are then conscious that they are free, because we would not diminish them, under any change of circumstances which can be anticipated. But a sinner daily resolves against the indulgences which he daily practises; and it is his love of the pleasures or the profits of iniquity, which stimulates him to pursue them. He loves the wages of sin, more than the riches and the honours of heaven. Where our treasures are, there will our hearts, our affections be also; and the treasures of a sinner, and his heart are in the lust which he obeys. This is the second illustration which we proposed of our text.

In the 3d place, sin enslaves the will. "The will is that state of the mind, which is previous to, and which causes, those actions, which we call voluntary, or free." It is true, that a sinner acts by choice, equally as the most pious of men; that is, he is free to do the evil which he loves. But is he free also to do good? "Out of thine own mouth will I judge thee, thou wicked servant." You love the course of evil into which you have entered; you choose it; but should you not rather be upright, than dishonest; of a generous and forgiving, than of a malignant temper? Should you not rather be benevolent, than envious and selfish? humble, than proud? temperate, than devoted to the gratifications of appetite? chaste in your affections and conduct, than licentious and impure? Why then do you persist in vices, which you know must at last overwhelm you with shame and misery? You daily acknowledge that you *cannot* abandon them. You daily practise them, as a slave thoughtlessly goes to the task, to which he has been so long accustomed, that his motions in performing it are almost mechanical. You have a thousand times resolved that you would reform; but your continuance in sin demonstrates the moral impotence of your will. Say not then that you are free, because you act from choice; because you have invented excuses, or even justifications of your conduct. These excuses, these justifications, are but suggestions of your sinful passions, to conceal from you the thraldom in which you are held. "When you would do good, evil is present with you;" and notwithstanding all the means and motives which are applied to dissuade you from vice, and to encourage you to virtue and holiness; notwithstanding your convictions of duty, and of the ultimate happiness which it will produce, you persist in errour and iniquity. Your will bows submissive to the authority of your passions, while reason and religion stand pleading with you to be wise, to reform, and to be happy forever. Is not he then who committeth sin completely the servant of sin?

But it is said, if the soul be thus enslaved, is man accountable for the actions which he cannot control? Yes; for however debased be his condition, he was once free, and voluntarily became a slave. He freely sold his faculties to the service of taskmasters, who he knew never relented; whose bondage, he was taught by the experience of thousands, was as strong and more cruel than the grave. God never formed an accountable being, with propensities to evil which he could not resist. There is a season of life, in which every passion may be subjected. If at this season we indulge its demands, its authority soon becomes too strongly confirmed to be easily shaken. We begin with prescribing bounds, within which we will limit evil gratifications. We pass these bounds. We resolve to be more circumspect; but at the same time excuse our guilt, by pleading the strength of temptation. The same temptations recur, or we are excited by others of equal force, and we *justify* that, which before we attempted only to *excuse*. Then is the soul enslaved. But who will say, that the first, or the second transgression was necessary? that the temptation, by no exertion, could be resisted? Whatever be the power of any propensity to evil, who is not conscious of a time, when he might have obtained over it an easy and complete victory? Not only for his guilty conduct, therefore, is the sinner accountable, but for the very strength of the passion by which he was excited to commit it; for that very state of the mind, by which he was predisposed to become the slave of temptation. This is indeed an awful consideration. It is a consideration which, duly influencing the mind, would induce the sinner, not only to hazard every comfort of life, but life itself, in the endeavour, to repent, to reform, and to become holy.

But though man be not able, of himself, to overcome the impotence of the enslaved affections and will; yet by the means of grace with which he is furnished, he may regain his liberty, and become a child of God. "My grace is sufficient for thee; my strength is made perfect in weakness." God is accessible at all times, and in all places, by prayer. He has made his will so plain, that he who runs may read; and he has enforced it by motives, which to serious and ingenuous minds, seem irresistible. There is therefore no excuse for guilt. For the greatest sinners there is hope, because there are means of reformation, which, wisely applied, will be effectual. Behold then the goodness and the severity of God; and let it lead us to repentance.

By these considerations we justify the dreadful denunciations of the gospel against those, who are confirmed in the love and practice of evil. They have resisted means of grace, and motives to piety and virtue, which our Lord assures us would have converted those idolatrous and abandoned cities, which were overwhelmed and destroyed by the vengeance of God. They have freely and habitually debased all the powers of their souls, when they knew that, thus perverted, and thus corrupted, they could have no interest in the promises. The temptations, to which they have yielded their piety and virtue, were designed to exercise and to strengthen their holy and benevolent affections; and if they had been vigorously resisted, success would have been certain, and the honours and rewards of victory splendid and great. What then does not he deserve who has sold himself a slave to vice, notwithstanding the convictions of his guilt, the reproaches of conscience, and the admonitions, the promises, and threatenings of the gospel; who has slighted the presence of God, been unaffected by his holiness, regardless of his justice, and ungrateful for his love? What means, what motives would reclaim a sinner, on whom the excitements of christianity are unavailing? They who refused Moses' law died without mercy. Of how much sorer punishment then shall not he be thought worthy, who has trodden under foot the Son of God, and counted the blood of the covenant an unholy thing, and done despite to the spirit of grace?

But God never abandons one, who has not completely abandoned himself. If you feel, therefore, one emotion of godly sorrow, you may receive pardon and life, for you *may* repent and reform. I beseech you then in Christ's stead, be ye reconciled to God.

DISCOURSE III.

*Work out your own salvation with fear and trembling;
for it is God that worketh in you both to will and to
do of his good pleasure.*

THE text contains both a doctrine and
a duty. The duty is, that we work out
our own salvation with fear and trembling;
the doctrine, that it is God who worketh
in us to will and to do of his good pleasure.
Between them there is a close and very
important relation, though they are apparently contradictory. I would obviate this
apparent inconsistency, and illustrate their
relation; and, by the powerful and interesting motives which they involve, urge you
to become workers together with God, in
securing your final and eternal happiness.

It is a fundamental principle in all our reasonings on the communications or the operations of God, so far as they respect mankind, that he does and must act in perfect consistency with the natures which he has given us. We are rational, and he therefore addresses our reasons, requiring faith no further than he furnishes evidence to support it. We are free, and he therefore proposes good and evil to our choice. The supposition is absurd, that an infinitely wise and good Being would give a command to a creature, which he could not obey; that he would offer salvation on a condition with which the creature could not comply, and then condemn him for not complying with it. As the commands and promises and threatenings of the gospel are therefore addressed to all, either the gospel is not true, or man is entirely a free agent.—The supposition is absurd, that God would create man with a capacity of discriminating truth from errour, and virtue from vice, and then require a belief which directly contradicted his reason. It is true that God may reveal doctrines which are above our comprehensions, and, by the evidence that they are revealed by him, may convince us of their truth. But in this very evidence he addresses our reasons, and leaves us without excuse if we do not receive them. But it is impossible, while we exercise our reasons, to believe that God has commanded us to work out our own salvation with fear and trembling, and at the same time to believe, that we are dependent for our final happiness on his unconditional election; that unless we are thus elected, all our prayers and all our labours will be wholly ineffectual. It is to destroy all the obligations of piety, except on the elect. It is to annihilate the great doctrine of human responsibility; for they who are unconditionally elected, as they are perfectly secured from any fatal errour or vice, cannot properly be considered as responsible; nor can an account justly be demanded of men, with whatever means of religion they have been favoured, and with whatever motives to its practice, who were unconditionally doomed to destruction. These remarks are appropriate to the illustration which I propose of the text. The doctrine is one of the most interesting which the gospel proposes, "It is God who worketh in you both to will and to do of his good pleasure;" and it is in perfect consistency with the command, "work out your own salvation with fear and trembling."

God works in us, 1. by the influence of creation and providence; 2. by the influence of conscience; 3. by the influence of the divine word; 4. by the influence of prayer; and 5thly, by the influence of the holy spirit.

1. By the influence of creation and providence. "The heavens declare the glory of God, and the firmament sheweth his handy-work; day unto day uttereth speech, and night unto night sheweth knowledge of him." The minutest particle of matter is an evidence of a Creator, because no particle could create itself. Every evidence which is exhibited in every

object, of wisdom, of power, and of goodness, is an evidence of these attributes in God. Every adaptation of objects to one another, is a distinct proof of the providence of God. Reflect on the skill, which is displayed in the structure of a flower, a leaf, a spire of grass. It is unfathomable. It awakens admiration and reverence of its creator in every serious mind. Extend your views then to the whole vegetable creation. God is in all, and over all. Without him, not one could have existed, not one could exist for a moment. How well adapted are they therefore to keep in exercise the emotions which they awaken? Observe the minutest insect. How wonderful is its organization? The most admirable contrivance of man bears no comparison with it. How much more wonderful then is that wisdom,' which framed every individual of the vast variety of creatures which inhabit our globe? You see that every creature is suited to its element; that abundant provision is made for its wants, and that it possesses all the

means which are requisite for their gratification. Can you thus reflect on God,
without sentiments of gratitude and devotion? If we feel these sentiments in
reflecting on his creation and providence,
it is God working in us to will and to do
of his good pleasure. His agency is as
certain in producing these effects in our
hearts, as it is in the structure of our
hearts, or of the objects which we contemplate. Observe your own forms. Reflect
on your intellectual, your social, your moral
nature; your entire dependence, and the
constant goodness of God in sustaining
you; your unnumbered wants, and the
provision which is made for them; your
capacity of improvement, and the means
of attaining it. Are not each of these
most powerful motives to love, to adore,
and to obey all the will of your Creator?
The more we reflect on ourselves, the
deeper becomes our conviction, that in
God we live, and move, and have our
being; and in thus producing this conviction, does he not work in us to will and to

do of his good pleasure? All which is great and beautiful, all which is wise and beneficent in creation and providence, is exhibited to exercise our admiration, our reverence, our gratitude, our love; all which is mysterious, or afflictive, to try our faith and resignation. These sentiments and affections are essential to true piety; and if they are excited by a contemplation of his government or of his works, the agency of God in producing them is to be acknowledged and adored.

2. God works in us by the influence of conscience; that faculty by which we judge of the rectitude or impropriety of our conduct; which makes vice a source of unutterable anguish, and virtue productive of the highest happiness. So powerful is its influence, that to repress it, often baffles all the efforts of the most abandoned; and thousands daily feel its tortures, whose apparent prosperity we ignorantly envy. In an approving conscience does a good man find a refuge from all the oppressions of the world; a support under the heaviest

burden of adversity; an excitement to perseverance in duty, with whatever difficulties and dangers it may be attended. And if he whom conscience condemns would regard its admonitions, and submit to its restraints, virtue and peace would soon be restored in his heart. You must deny therefore, that God intended by this means to produce this effect, or acknowledge, that by every operation of conscience, he is working in us to will and to do of his good pleasure. If the joys of an approving, and the distresses of a wounded conscience, are sanctions of the will of God, which all acknowledge who believe that man is a subject of the divine government, then are they designed by him to co-operate with the revelation of his will, in producing that obedience which he demands. I appeal to your experience, if you have not been restrained by conscience from actions, which you were powerfully excited to perform; if its reproaches have not awakened repentance, and the most earnest desires and endeavours to love God more, and to serve him better. I appeal to your experience, if the consciousness of having discharged your duty, has not rendered you more resolute and vigorous in pursuing it; if it have not detached your affections from objects which are vain and vicious; consoled you in afflictions, and made you supremely happy in whatever you deemed the service of God. This is to will and to do of his good pleasure. It is what his word inculcates; and in every excitement of conscience, either to repentance or to increasing fidelity, is God as literally working in us, as if he personally suggested the motives by which we are actuated.

3. God operates upon our wills and upon our conduct, by the influence of his word. The gospel contains a perfect rule, suited to every condition of man, and to every circumstance of his life. To convince us that this is the will of God, on which depends our eternal condition in the future state, we have the evidence of prophecy and of miracles. It is indeed a

rule of life, which instantly approves itself
to every unprejudiced mind, and he that
doeth his will, will know of the doctrine
that it is from God; but can it be doubted
that these evidences were designed to
confirm our faith and to *secure* our obedience, and thus to work in us both to will
and to do of his good pleasure? They
who saw and heard our Lord, but rejected
his authority, were condemned, because
they did not yield to the influence of these
powerful motives to faith and holiness.
"Wo unto thee, Corazin; wo unto thee,
Bethsaida; for if the mighty works had
been done in Tyre and Sidon, which have
been done in thee, they would have re-
pented long ago in sackcloth and ashes."
But why did they deserve condemnation,
if these miracles were not intended to work
in them faith and obedience? It was not
by an arbitrary and irresistible impulse,
that God then produced conviction of the
truth of the gospel, and that devotion to
him which he required. To convince and
to convert his hearers, our Lord referred

to the prophecies, and to the works which he had wrought in his Father's name; and that they were adapted to produce faith and repentance, thanks to God, is evinced by the happy experience of millions. For the same purpose did our Lord enforce his requirements, by the most glorious promises and the most awful threatenings. He places before us happiness and misery, heaven and hell, and then bids us choose the service of God or of sin. He works in us to will and to do of his good pleasure, by the most affecting motives which could possibly be proposed to rational beings; by the holy example which he exhibited for our imitation; by his sufferings and death, to obtain the forgiveness of the sins of which we repent; and if we will not receive the evidence of Moses and the prophets, of Christ and the apostles; if we are not excited by this evidence, nor by his promises and denunciations, to the holiness which he demands, we should not be persuaded, though one rose from the dead. Could more be done, consistently with the freedom of man, to secure our faith, and the entire submission of our own to his perfect will?

4. God works in us to will and to do of his good pleasure, by the influence of prayer; an influence of which every pious heart is deeply sensible; which naturally results from a sense of the august presence of that Being, to whom prayer is addressed; from that deep sensibility which is then experienced, of his eternity, his power, his holiness, his goodness and his truth; from the deep conviction which is then felt, of our own, and of the entire and constant dependence of all creatures upon him. He works in us *to pray*, by teaching us our relation to him as children, his readiness to hear and to bless us, and his gracious purposes toward us in another and a better world. Is it possible thus to approach God, without the deepest reverence, love, gratitude, humility, and resignation? Is it possible, at the same time, to derive our happiness from this intercourse, to retain the sentiments which it inspires, and to

find pleasure in indulgences, which are forbidden in the gospel? We know the influence of intercourse with the wise and good. Admiration of their virtues naturally and easily leads us to a desire of imitation. We are ready and happy to do much, to retain their confidence and affection. We are encouraged to perseverance, by all which they have done, and all which they have enjoyed in consequence of their virtue. Nay, the presence of the wise and good awes even the most vicious; and they cannot endure their society, because it confirms their consciousness of guilt. How much more effectual will be the influence of intercourse with God? Who would be dishonest, revengeful, impure, avaricious, or proud; who would omit duties which he acknowledges, and commit offences against which he is repeatedly and most solemnly warned, if he felt the presence of God, if he were accustomed to that communion with Him, to which he is encouraged in the gospel? In admitting us then, to this intercourse, does not God work in

us to will and to do of his good pleasure?
Does not the close, the natural connexion
of the cause with the effect, demonstrate
that prayer was appointed by God, as one
of the means of qualifying us for the eternal enjoyments of his kingdom?

5. God works in us by the agency of
his holy spirit. It is well known that the
holy spirit descended on the apostles on
the day of pentecost, by the influence of
which they were enabled to preach the
gospel to every people in their own language, and to perform the most wonderful
miracles in confirmation of their doctrine.
It is obvious, that the holy spirit for which
we are encouraged to pray, cannot be the
same gift which was conferred, for most
important purposes, on the first preachers
of the New Testament. Yet the influence
of the spirit we are taught to expect, if
with a suitable disposition we seek for it;
and do we not receive it, in the sentiments
of religious admiration, gratitude, love and
devotion, which a contemplation of his
works and government inspire? in the

restraints and encouragements of conscience? in the divine light which the
gospel pours over the soul, which feels its
power and yields to its motives; in the
holy affections which it awakens; the consolation which it produces in affliction;
the strength and delight which it furnishes
in the service of God? Do we not receive
the spirit of God in the exercise of prayer,
when we feel that our prayers have increased our confidence in God; fanned the
flame of our love; rendered us more humble and vigilant; more deeply interested
in the good of others, and more active to
promote it; more detached from the world,
more happy in the hope of heaven, and
more zealous to attain it? The spirit acts
by the agency of means; and we receive
the spirit by every means, by which our
love of God and of holiness is increased.
By his spirit, therefore he acts upon our
wills, in perfect consistency with their
freedom. He has promised his holy spirit
to those only who ask, who seek for it.

Does not the doctrine, thus illustrated,

most powerfully enforce the command, work out your own salvation with fear and trembling? What encouragement would induce us to labour for our eternal happiness, to use with fidelity and gratitude the means which are appointed of securing an interest in the great redemption, if we are unaffected by the assurance, that God is thus working in us to will and to do of his good pleasure? The apostles, in preaching the gospel, and in persuading men to receive and obey it, are called workers together with God; and we are workers together with God in effectuating our own salvation, when we improve as we ought the means of grace, the price which is put into our hands to obtain wisdom, and pardon, and life.

To work out our own salvation, we must then, in the first place, habitually acknowledge God in his works, and in his government of the world. In vain would be all the displays which are presented in creation and providence, of the power, the wisdom, and the goodness of God, if there were none capable of contemplating them, of learning the character, and performing the will of their author; and God has given us the capacities which are requisite for these purposes, that by thus knowing him, we may be excited to diligence in his service. We have only to open our eyes, and we shall see God, every where active and every where good. We have only to open our hearts, and we shall feel our dependence and obligations; the most perfect confidence and entire submission.

> ...."Full often, it is true,
> "Our wayward intellect, the more we learn
> "Of nature, overlooks her Author more."
>
> *Task*, B. 3.

But that the contemplation of his works and providence is adapted to awaken the most elevated sentiments of piety, and to animate us in the service of God, is known to all who have ever seriously thought of God. To derive from them these effects, we must habitually refer to God all the wisdom, power, and benevolence which they discover; we must habitually remember that he is in all, and over all; we must daily acknowledge his government, both in the prosperous and adverse events of life; and whether they affect others or ourselves. Is it a hard requirement, that we thus cherish a remembrance of God, and all the sentiments and virtues which this sense of his presence and perfections will inspire? In his sermon on the mount, our Saviour taught his disciples thus to seek God, and to cherish the gratitude, the confidence and devotion which he required. Behold the flowers of the field! Solomon in all his glory was not arrayed like one of these. Will not he then, who has clothed the flowers with so much beauty, clothe you also, O ye of little faith? Behold the fowls of the air. They neither sow, nor reap, nor gather into barns; yet your heavenly father feedeth them. Will he not then feed you? Do you not see in his care of the creatures about you, a motive to love him, to trust in him, and to serve him? Thus keep the Lord ever before you, by an habitual regard to his creation and providence, by that confidence in him and that gratitude which he thus inculcates, and by that submission which you owe to Him on whom you are entirely dependent, and you so far obey the command, "to work out your salvation with fear and trembling."   Every reference which is thus made to his presence, every sentiment of love and devotion which is thus excited, qualifies us at once for a better improvement of every other means of grace, and for the final happiness for which they are all intended to prepare us.

2. We work out our own salvation, when we avail ourselves of the encouragements and admonitions of conscience; when we are prompted by the happiness which results from a consciousness of having performed our duties, to increased earnestness in the service of God; and when, by the reproaches of a wounded spirit, we are induced to repentance and reformation. It was for these purposes that God implanted the faculty within us; and he who disregards the suggestions of

conscience, by whatever circumstance it is excited, refuses to co-operate with God in the great work of salvation. By our disregard of conscience, its influence becomes gradually repressed ; and hence its inefficiency. But if we cherished, as we should, the delightful emotions which are excited by a hope of the favour of God, how strong would be its impulse to increasing holiness? If, whenever we are made conscious of guilt, we reflected maturely on the design of God in thus awakening us ; and on the nature and just consequences of our sins ; if we were reminded, as we should be by our sufferings, that without repentance and a renewed heart we cannot see God and live, then should we be guilty of no habitual transgression. The restraints and encouragements of conscience have been partially felt by all ; but if we would make them subservient to our attainment of the great salvation, we must regard every suggestion of this heavenly monitor ; we must endeavour to maintain a conscience void of offence, toward God, and toward man.

3. We work out our own salvation, when we attend to the evidences of the truth of the gospel; when we study it with frequency and earnestness, to ascertain what is the will of God; when we make its requirements our supreme rule, and cherish its hopes, as infinitely the best possession of man. As God is there working in us by the force of these evidences, by his promises and denunciations, by the beauty of holiness as it is illustrated in the example of Christ, and by the infinite mercy which is expressed in his death, we become workers together with him, in cherishing our faith, in conforming to his ordinances, in obeying his laws, and in submitting to his appointments, trusting in his promises. To know the will of God, does not indeed require labour. He who runs may read it. The wayfaring man, though a fool, need not err therein. But to *retain its influence* on our hearts and lives, demands our utmost exertions; and one of the most efficient means of securing it, is the daily and attentive study of the divine word;

the habitual remembrance, that this is the law by which we shall ultimately be judged. Every one who knows any thing of the deceitfulness of his own heart, feels the necessity of this constant reference to the word of God, to guide and to guard him; and by every hour of its serious study, by every recurrence to it as our rule of life, by every conformity to its institutions and obedience to its requirements, from a principle of love to God, do we advance toward the great salvation, the inheritance of its promises.

4. As God works in us to will and to do of his good pleasure, by the influence of prayer, so do we become workers together with God, when we live in the habit of intimate and devout communion with him. We are expressly taught, that much of that happiness in the future world which is involved in the promised salvation, will be derived from intercourse with God in prayer. In this world, it is one of the most efficient means of that holiness, of which it will be the eternal security in the

future. All the exhibitions which God has given of himself, all his promises, all our weaknesses, and wants, and fears, are motives by which God is working in us to pray. If they produce on us the effects for which they are intended, if they excite us to pray, then do we thus work out our own salvation. Every prayer, offered with deep humility and reverence, and love and resignation, renders us better prepared for that union with God, in which will consist the glory of the saints in heaven; and so far will be these motives by which God is working in us, from promoting our salvation, if we are not thus excited to habitual and devout communion with him, that they will justly become the causes to us of the severest condemnation.

5. We work out our own salvation, when we seek the influences of the Spirit of God, and are actuated by them; the influence of that spirit which lives and addresses us in all the works of God; which impels or restrains us by the agency of conscience; which pervades the divine

word, giving efficacy to its sacred truths; which descends upon the sincere worshipper in the exercise of prayer. It is a spirit which God will give to all who seek it; which he is more ready to confer, than is the kindest parent to bestow bread upon his hungry offspring. How perfectly consistent then is this influence of God, with the freedom of the human will? Every sentiment of piety and virtue, which is excited by the works and providence of God, by conscience, by the study of the word of God, or by prayer, is to be attributed to the Spirit of God. Every emotion of repentance, every desire of greater devotion, is to be ascribed to the strivings of his spirit. By them *he* is working in *us*. By cherishing these fruits of the spirit, we co-operate with God, in securing for ourselves glory, and honour, and immortality.

The requirement to fear and tremble in the great work of salvation, does not imply, that we should engage in the service of God with a constant dread of his displeasure; that by our exposure to fall, we should be rendered timid in the discharge of duty. No. Whenever life is represented as a warfare, we are exhorted to a courage which no dangers can daunt; and the apostle who has recorded the requirement, that we "work out our salvation with fear and trembling," was one of the most fearless and heroick of mankind. But our care, our watchfulness will always be increased, in proportion to our estimation of the object which we would attain; and surely, if we are sensible of the worth of that salvation which is proffered in the gospel, if we realize our weakness, if we reflect on the tendency of our passions to evil, and the number and strength of the temptations to which we are exposed, we shall be incessantly *cautious;* and though not timid in reflecting on the labours which are to be accomplished, we shall, above all things, *be afraid to sin.* It is this fear indeed, which distinguishes true courage from that impetuosity of temper, that unprincipled hardihood of mind, which the unthinking and the vicious mistake for magnanimity. We cannot have just sentiments of the salvation which awaits us, if we are not faithful to the service of God; of the duties which he requires; of the relapses of others from virtue and piety; of our own frequent transgressions, and of the awful consequences of sin; and not fear, lest we should be overcome of evil. He who knows not this dread of sin, has no just conceptions of the worth of that redemption, which is offered to us by the Son of God.

Considering then that God is working in us to will and to do of his good pleasure, let us be encouraged to work out our own salvation with fear and trembling; to fear lest, a promise being left of entering into rest, any of us should fall short of it. Labour not for the meat which perisheth, but for that meat which endureth unto everlasting life. Diligently apply to every means of grace, and God will give them efficacy. He has never said to one of the children of men, *Seek ye me*, in vain. Ask then, and it shall be given you; seek and ye shall find; knock and it shall be opened to you; for if ye, being evil, know how to give good gifts to your children, will not your heavenly Father give his holy spirit to them that ask him?—Bestow on us this spirit, holy Father! Guide us by thy counsel, secure us by thy grace, and receive us at last to the perfect and eternal enjoyment of thee, through Jesus Christ, to whom be glory for ever. AMEN.

DISCOURSE IV.

All things whatsoever ye would that men should do to you, do ye even so to them.

THE text is a summary of the duties of social morality. It is a rule of life which, if habitually applied, would supersede the necessity of innumerable laws; for it is adapted to repress the worst passions, to awaken and to exercise every good affection, and to diffuse through our own minds, through our families, and through society, all the improvement and happiness of which social virtue can be productive. *Whatsoever ye would that men should do to you, do ye even so to them.*

The precept is deeply founded in the nature of man. Without some regard to justice and to benevolence, society could not have existed; and so many are the weaknesses and the wants of which all are sensible, and so wretched must every one have found himself, without the consideration and regard of those about him, that we are not surprised at meeting with this requirement, in the works of many, who not only lived long before the gospel, but who were wholly ignorant of each other.* But in ten thousand instances have men been actuated by it from a strong sentiment

---

*This great rule is implied in a speech of Lycias, and expressed in distinct phrases by Thales and Pictacus; and I have seen it, word for word, in the original of Confucius. It has been usual for zealous men to ridicule and abuse all those who dare on this point to quote the Chinese philosopher. But instead of supporting their cause, they would shake it, if it could be shaken, by their uncandid asperity; for they ought to remember, that one great end of revelation, as it is most expressly declared, was not to instruct the wise and few, but the many and unenlightened. To millions of the Chinese, who toil for their daily support, it is unknown even at this day; nor, was it known ever so perfectly, would it have a divine sanction with the multitude.—*Sir W. Jones. Asiatick Researches V.4. p.* 177.

See also Grotius on the text.

of benevolence, who never thought of it as
a law. For all the advantages therefore,
which are derived from the reception of it
as a divine command, and for the diffusion
of a knowledge of it through all classes of
men, we are indebted to the gospel; and
it is not necessary to take a wide survey of
life to be sensible, that, for these advantages, our obligations are unspeakably
great to the Author and Finisher of our
faith.

Such is the attachment of man to his
own person, opinions, and interest, as often
to render him insensible, or inconsiderate
of the feelings, sentiments, and interests
of others. The love of ourselves is natural; and so far is christianity from re-
proving the passion, that it makes our
self-love the standard by which we are to
regulate our love to our neighbour. But
between self-love and selfishness there is
an essential and important distinction. He
who loves his neighbour, as he loves himself, will never be selfish. But our self-
love degenerates into selfishness, in exact

proportion as it predominates over the love which we owe to others. A christian is bound, under all circumstances, to do to others, as he knows it is the duty, and as he might reasonably expect of others to do to him. Actuated by this great law, his self-love will impel him to every office of equity and of kindness. It is a law, in the application of which no ingenuous mind can be mistaken; and by which alone we might, without difficulty, determine the manner in which we ought to act, in every condition, relation, and circumstance of life.

The gospel makes our self-love the standard, by which we are to regulate our love to our neighbour. This is evidently the spirit of the text, as it is also of the second commandment of our Lord, *thou shalt love thy neighbour as thyself.* But the inquiry naturally arises, what is comprehended in that self-love which the gospel approves, and which it makes the measure by which we are to determine the extent of our social obligations. In Answering this inquiry, and in applying it, we illustrate and enforce the duties which are inculcated in the text.

There is a regard which every man may reasonably attach to his own person, to his own sentiments or opinions, to his interest and to his reputation; and this attachment naturally excites a wish, and an expectation of the regard of others. Now whatever we might reasonably expect of others, that it is our duty, on all occasions to practise; and to ascertain the extent of this obligation, it is necessary, in imagination, to exchange conditions with others, and to ask ourselves, what regard does the letter, or the spirit of the gospel require, that in such circumstances, we should receive from those about us? The inquiry, when seriously proposed, immediately receives the same answer from all.

1. We remark the influence of self-love on the protection and care of our own persons. To defend them from injuries, and to relieve their sufferings, are among the most interesting objects of our cares

and our pursuits; and often do they receive protection and comfort from others, which neither our own skill nor exertions could obtain. This universal dependence of men on one another, resulting from the weakness of every individual, and his liability to suffer without assistance, is the strongest bond of our social union; and we therefore reasonably expect from others a respect for our persons, and a readiness to defend and to assist us, so far as our conditions demand protection and aid. The duties of others to ourselves are not, indeed, for a moment, doubted by any. Self-love is always awake, and in an instant suggests and enforces them by innumerable and irresistible motives. But are not the same duties to others equally incumbent on us, and enforced by as many and as powerful considerations? Let us candidly apply the rule, and ingenuously admit the conclusions to which it leads us.

We have no right to expect from others an equal love of our persons, and an equal interest in their welfare, as we feel for them ourselves; but we do reasonably expect that no one, without provocation, will injure them. We often expect, when we have injured others, that the evil will not be retaliated. Let these expectations govern our conduct towards others, and every one will be secure, in his person, against injuries from those with whom he has intercourse. All have a right to demand, and God will require of us, a regard to their persons, proportioned to these requisitions which self-love makes for ourselves;—that is, not only that we refrain from inflicting suffering, but that we habitually exercise the mildness and forbearance of the christian temper; not only that we exert ourselves to avoid giving pain, but that we avail ourselves of every opportunity of alleviating distress. The person of another is as dear to him as ours is to us, and by exchanging conditions with him, our duties instantly become obvious. Is he in danger? Fly to rescue him, and submit to the inconvenience or hazard which *you* would require? Is he afflicted with disease?   Let the unwearied attention and uninterrupted kindness which you would wish to receive, be the measure by which to decide the kindness and attention which you owe to him.   Is he naked?   Is he hungry?   You would wish, you would expect, if in this condition to be fed and clothed.   Give freely then, of your bread, to those who need it, and comfortable raiment to him who is destitute.   Remember that thou mayest be a stranger, and receive cheerfully into thy house him who has no habitation; or who, far from his home, needs the shelter or the comforts which thou canst furnish.   You have, perhaps, wanted the care, the sympathy, the beneficence which others demand of you.   You *may* want them, even from those who now need, and implore your assistance.   If these considerations do not awaken our regard for others, we are affected by a selfishness altogether inconsistent with the gospel.

2.   To the variety of sentiments which exist among men we are referred, as another source of numerous and important

relative duties. This diversity is apparent, not only when we speak of religion and of civil policy, but in almost every subject on which we converse; and in proportion to the strength of our conviction of the rectitude of our opinions, we must be convinced that those of others, who differ from us, are erroneous. This application of the rule requires us to remember, that the persuasion of another may be as firm as ours; and consequently, that he may demand the same openness to conviction, which we should expect from himself. It requires us to realize, that the sentiments of another may appear to him as valuable and as important, as ours are to us, and to exercise towards him the charity, which *he* thinks that we need from himself. These are indeed sentiments, the tendency of which is so obviously evil, that we may reasonably doubt the correctness of the character of a man who avows them. Yet as we know that calumny and oppression irritate, rather than quiet the mind, and confirm instead of changing our opinions it is a violation of the plainest social duties to revile and to persecute. An uncandid, and uncharitable, a censorious and an over-bearing temper, is the result of ignorance of our own liability to errour; for they never were, and never will be indulged by those, who so judge others, as they would them-selves be judged.

What an effect would this application of the text produce upon our own, and the virtue and happiness of society? More than half of the diversity of sentiments in religion, in politicks, and in the business of life, is maintained by a spirit of opposi-tion, which is excited by our self-ignorance; and so generally are men ignorant of them-selves, and of course, so ready for opposi-tion, that a few ambitious, restless, and bigoted spirits, can easily keep the whole world in commotion. Many of the most distinguished promoters of this contrariety of opinions, and of this spirit of opposition, have no value for any sentiments, but as they may be rendered subservient to their own interests; and many, who think that they differ most widely, if brought together, and persuaded ingenuously to express their sentiments, would find, either that the difference between them existed only in their imaginations; or at most, that it was too inconsiderable to justify suspicion and enmity. There is indeed a real difference in the opinions of men, and there must be, while human nature remains as it is. But let men do to others as they would that others should do to them, and the order and happiness of society would not be so often interrupted; contention and strife would not be so frequent as they now are. If we were as candid and as charitable to others, as we would have them be to us, we should hear none of those slanderous reports, those false interpretations of the words or conduct of others, which originate in, and are circulated to gratify the worst passions; a thousand walls of separation between man and man would be broken down; and our progress would be rapid to that unity of spirit, and that perfection of

17

love, in which essentially consists the kingdom of Christ.

3. Every man desires the respect of others for his own *character*. The happiness of almost every one is essentially affected by the estimation in which he is held by those with whom he associates, or to whom he was known. In this application of the rule to far the greatest part of mankind, we might require only, that they treat the characters of others with the same tenderness which they would wish for *themselves*, if their own defects or vices were equally known to the world. We may, and should endeavour to know the characters of men, that we may know how to conduct our intercourse with them; that we may duly appreciate the virtuous, defend the injured, and be excited ourselves to increasing vigilance;—but let him who is without sin cast the first stone; let him only condemn without mercy, who needs not the mercy of God for himself; let conscience sit as judge in the court of our own minds, before we pronounce the sentence

of reprobation upon others. If you have
not committed crimes as great as have been
committed by others, consider that, under
similar circumstances, you *might* have been
guilty of them;—consider that, strong as
you now stand, you are *liable* to fall; and
place yourself in the condition of him, of
whom you are tempted to speak with contempt or with reproach. How do you wish
to be viewed or treated by others, when
you have done wrong, or have incurred
suspicion? The same gentleness and candour you are required to exercise. These
dispositions you will exercise, if you know
your own weakness, your evil propensities,
and your sins.

In determining the respect which we owe
to men in the different ranks of life, let us
place ourselves in their conditions. Have
you a servant? If you stood in the relation
to him which he does to you, you would desire, you would love a spirit of kindness
and of accommodation, and punctuality in
the discharge of pecuniary obligations. So
conduct towards him, and you will not only

promote his happiness, but secure his fidelity. Are you a servant? Ask, then, what you would have a right to require, if you were a master; and be as considerate of the interests of him whom you serve, as if they were your own. As a citizen, exercise the subordination, the deference to the laws, which you might reasonably wish of others, if you had been appointed to rule; and in all the relations and intercourses of life, estimate the tenderness and respect which are due, by that which you are conscious, in the same circumstances, you might consistently require. Honour others, as you would in their situations be honoured. Judge them as favourably as you would be judged. Defend them, when they are calumniated, with the same benevolent spirit with which you would wish to be vindicated. Then no parent would have reason to complain of his child, no friend of the desertion of him whom he loved, and no neighbour of the censoriousness of those about him;—no master would have occasion to reproach his servant, and no servant to blame his master ;—no magistrate would issue an unjust law, and no subject would rebel against the wise administration of the government of his country. If this single law of the gospel were universally a rule of life, we might, without suspicion, entrust our reputations to others, and form and enjoy every relation, without fear of any other disappointment, than death might occasion. Happy state of society! Blessed effects of the gospel! When will this confidence, this candour, this fidelity, this condescension and love prevail among men?

4. We are directed also to make our regard for *our own interests*, and the attention which we reasonably require to them, a measure by which to regulate our own regard to *the interests of others*. Who does not instantly anticipate the consequences of this application of the rule?

We would that men should be honest, where our interests are involved, and we deem it reasonable to demand an unreserved uprightness. But if our judgments are unperverted by selfishness, this expectation of honesty in others, this clear discernment of their duties, will render our own equally perceptible, and equally obligatory. Preserve this integrity then in all your dealings, and you will so far fulfil the law. We can have no better security of uprightness, than the certainty that any one will conduct towards us with the fairness, which he would wish for himself; for as no one is willing to be deceived, no one would then be guilty of deception. But is this the principle on which business is transacted? Look into the world. With what jealous caution are contracts made; and how many bonds, independent of the honour of man, are deemed requisite, as securities that engagements will be accomplished? It seems to be an established maxim, to do to others, as we think that others *would* do to us; and this maxim is so early and so impressively inculcated, that many, who are otherwise virtuous, appear to mistake this for the requirement of Christ. But it is a very different standard to which he requires his disciples to conform their conduct. However corrupt others may be, to be christians, we must do to them, as, in the sincerity and piety of our hearts, we wish that they should do to us.

Innumerable opportunities occur, in which we may essentially aid the interests of others, or protect them from injury. We sometimes witness, or experience these beneficent offices, and they always attach us to him who performs them. These occasions of applying the text cannot be specified. They occur every day ; and *He* who observes the falling of a sparrow to the ground, will not be regardless of the man, who will turn out of his way to suggest to his neighbour an improvement which might be made ; or be delayed for a moment, that he may mend a gap, by which the field of another, when he was unconscious of it, was exposed to injury.

This is one of the great laws by which we shall be judged at the bar of Christ. In this short compass has our divine teacher expressed all the duties, which he requires from man to man; and as no one is so ignorant that he cannot understand this law; as no memory is so treacherous that it cannot retain it, all will be without excuse by whom it is disregarded. A narrow, selfish spirit, is of all others the most inconsistent with the gospel. Be ye therefore kind and affectionate one towards another; and as ye would that men should do to you, do ye even so to them. Forgive, because God has commanded it, and because ye feel your frailty, and ye shall be forgiven. Give, and it shall be given to you. Bear ye one another's burdens, and so fulfil the law of Christ. Let your fidelity equal your highest desires of others; and let us consider every man as our brother, who has occasion for our integrity, or our kindness. By these social duties, and the pious and personal offices of the gospel, may we all be trained for an eternal union with the just made perfect, with the Redeemer, and with God!

DISCOURSE V.

Owe no man any thing, but to love one another.

ONE of the best means of maintaining that love of others, which christianity requires, is to owe them nothing but love. We owe love to all, because we are all mutually dependent, and there is no one whose sympathy or assistance we may not require ; because we are the offspring of the same parent, who made us to live together, and to love one another, as members of one family; because all are capable of immortal improvement and happiness. This love indeed will excite us to every exertion to relieve the wants of others,

18

and to extend to them every accommodation which, in similar circumstances, we should wish for ourselves; but the same love will impel him, who has received the favour, to that gratitude to his benefactor, and that kindness to others, which are the best returns for every office of benevolence; and where, by borrowing or purchasing, he has incurred the obligation to pay, it will render him not less solicitous and active to satisfy the just demands of his creditor, than, if he were the creditor, he should desire for himself.

Every duty growing out of our relations and intercourses is recognized in the gospel, and inculcated as a part of the service which we owe to God. This is a most important principle; and I would to God, my brethren, that it were deeply impressed upon all our minds. We are too apt to consider religion and morality as distinct and independent; and to believe that a man may have an incorruptible morality who has no piety, and that the prayers and conversations of some men stamp their characters with the impression of piety, while they have at best an uncertain, or perhaps an obviously defective morality. It is often this very erroneous sentiment, which occasions the intrusion of unhallowed members into the church; and it is the satisfaction with their own morality, which this sentiment awakens in others, which causes them to view with jealousy the professors of religion, and even to congratulate themselves in triumph, that they have made no acknowledgments of their faith and obligations. But let it be remembered, that every duty, growing out of our relations and intercourses, is as essentially a part of the service of God, as the study of his word, and the exercises of prayer. Let it be remembered, that then only do we *love God*, when we *keep his commandments;* that for all our sentiments, affections, and conduct, we shall be called into judgment; and that it is essential to our preparation for a union with the *just* made perfect, that we love and faithfully practise in this world the *righteousness* of the gospel. To one branch of this great law I invite your attention. "Owe no man any thing," says the word of God, "but to love one another."

The principle, from which results the obligation to the payment of debts, is obvious; and this obligation is as imperious, as any one in the whole range of social morality. A debt implies an equivalent, or a consideration, received by ourselves, or by some one for whose punctuality we have made ourselves responsible. The acknowledgment of a debt, therefore, is an acknowledgment that so much of our possessions as we owe to another, belongs of right to *him*, and no longer to ourselves. This right in his property, of every one to whom he is indebted, every good man feels; and therefore feels himself bound to the denial of every indulgence, which would interfere with the obligations into which he has entered with his creditor. He will deem his time and his labours to be in the right of his creditor, so far as they are necessary for the satisfaction of his just demand. This is both *law* and *gospel*. Christianity does not indeed sanction the oppression of the poor and unfortunate, whose necessities have been the unhappy cause of the obligations which they have contracted; or who, subsequently to the contraction of debts, have been involved in calamities which render payment impossible. Here the great law of doing to others, as we would that others should do to us, requires the exercise of all the forbearance, and tenderness, and accommodation, which we should wish for ourselves; but, in its turn, it demands of us all the efforts of our strength and skill, as speedily as possible, and to the extent of his rights, to satisfy him, whose forbearance and kindness we have experienced. Nor is the text to be interpreted as a prohibition, under any circumstances, to the contraction of debts. In civil society, this would be an impracticable command. But it plainly implies the duty of habitual caution not to owe, what we shall not be able to pay; to be punctual in our pecuniary engagements; and not to indulge in any expenses, or any modes of living, either inconsistent with this punctuality, or which will cause us to resort to debts for the maintainance of our stations. These duties, my brethren, will naturally flow from that love which christianity inculcates; and these duties I would enforce, by exhibiting some of the causes and the consequences of their neglect.

There are some men of that invincible *indolence*, that they are always willing to live upon others, while others can be induced by any means to support them; and what they cannot obtain from *charity*, they procure by *credit*, without feeling a sensation of uneasiness, till their little stock of honour, and the patience of those who have trusted them, are alike exhausted. An indolent man is satisfied, if his wants are supplied for the day which is passing over him; and with indolence is generally united that deeply rooted selfishness, which represses every consideration of the inconvenience, or the unhappiness which he may occasion to those who are relying on his integrity, and whose confidence he so easily abuses. Every debt thus contracted is in violation of the plainest principles of justice; and let a man make what professions he will, if he had rather borrow than labour, and owe another than support himself, he is without the pale of the church, and so far forfeits his relation to Christ. "This also," says Paul, "we commanded, if a man will not work, neither shall he eat."

But indolence is not the only cause of the contraction of unjust debts. There are some men, who are not only active, but of a zeal in their pursuits which forbids every prudential consideration. They have ever some favourite project in operation, of the accomplishment of which they are certain; some castle in the air, for which they have yet to provide *a foundation;* and as these are not, commonly, men who have enriched themselves by their enterprises, they are obliged to depend on others, to whom they can make their projects *almost* as reasonable as to themselves; and who are promised, if they will provide the foundation, the castle and all its riches may easily become their own. In this source have innumerable debts originated; and by this cause have many, in their eagerness to swell a competency into a fortune, been stripped of all their possessions, and over-whelmed with wretchedness.

This disposition to new and untried schemes, is generally a cause of misfortune, alike to him who forms, and to those who adopt them. Enterprise and improvements should indeed be encouraged; but there is a wide difference between a mind which calmly investigates principles, and shews their results; and which applies its skill to the diminution of human labour, to the advancement of the knowledge of man, and the increase of the comforts of life; and the wild suggestions of an undisciplined imagination, which fancies a work which is anticipated to be half accomplished; or the uncurbed designs of men, anxious to ac-quire fortunes in a day, and regardless who are disappointed and ruined, if they are elevated and enriched. Of such designs have many unsuspecting individuals, many virtuous families become the victims; and he who would avoid debt, and all its distressing consequences, must avoid, as a certain means of inducing it, both the love of forming projects, and the indiscreet adoption of the schemes of the visionary.

Another cause of iniquitous debts, is *extravagance*, induced by the love of pomp or of pleasure; the habit of indulging freely in expence, without considering its tendencies. To have the means of indulging this expence, is all which some men desire; and they think as little of the obligation which has been given for what has been received, as if a word at any moment might cancel it. This is barefaced fraud and knavery. Perhaps indeed the mask of business is assumed to cover the deception. But the man who indulges his appetites, or his vanity, or any other passion, at the expence of others who rely on his integrity, and squanders the property which he obtained with the pretence of improving it, should be treated as the enemy of virtue and of social order. It is in the habits of such men that most of the suspicion originates, which so strongly marks the intercourses of business. They injure all who confide in them, and corrupt all with whom they have intercourse.

There are likewise men, who, without all this vice, essentially violate the great principles of justice, in their habitual neglect of pecuniary obligations. Some, from the mere gratification of retaining property in their possession, avail themselves of every artifice to delay the satisfaction of demands, the right of which they acknowledge. This is an indisputable evidence of a contracted, a selfish and sordid mind. Others are not less negligent in the discharge of this important duty, from utter inconsideration. Property *in their possession*, becomes *their own ;* and having appropriated it to the purposes for which it was obtained, they think no more of him who may claim it, nor are aware at all of the disappointment which awaits them.   Some very freely contract debts, which they *hope*, and *flatter themselves*, they shall be enabled to pay, without perhaps having any proper basis on which to build the expectation; and others, having escaped in a few instances the effects which they apprehended, have been emboldened to perseverance, till they have involved themselves in ruin.   All these causes, in a greater or less degree, are to be attributed to a deficiency of moral and religious principle; to a neglect of the great duty of doing to others, as we would that they should do to us; and to inconsideration of the account which we must all ultimately render, when the neglect or violation of integrity towards man, will be accounted unrighteousness towards God.   In these causes originate very much of the vice and misery of life.

We have said that, to this dishonesty is to be ascribed the jealousies, which so strongly mark all the intercourses of business.   Many who felt not the cravings of avarice, nor any solicitude for the pomp of wealth; who commenced their career of life with the best resolutions of uprightness, and who long and firmly maintained them, by the deceptions, the impositions which they have experienced, have been seduced to the same disingenuousness and duplicity, and become as vile as those by whom they were corrupted. Are not the instigators of this vice, then, in the sight of God, accountable for its consequences?

To trust an honest, but necessitous man, is one of the most grateful offices of life. It is a privilege for which they owe much to God, who are permitted to enjoy it. But how often are even the most upright, objects of suspicion, simply because men have been so often deceived, that they know not how to repose confidence in one another. This unhappy influence, produced upon the minds of the rich, and which hasty and uncandid observers attribute in every instance to parsimony, is more frequently than we are aware to be attributed to a profligate dishonesty in many whom they have trusted. Unable to discriminate, by the professions of men, between the virtuous and the base, they sometimes treat the base as virtuous, and deny their confidence and aid to the integrity, which if better known, would be prized and honoured. Let the condemnation therefore, which is excited by this disappointment and suffering of the upright, fall where it is due; upon those who break obligations with as much facility as they break their bread; and who regard not the miseries which they occasion to others, if they may gratify their passions, and enjoy the day as it passes them.

A man who indulges himself in contracting debts, if he had it not before, generally acquires with this indulgence a habit of forming and of pursuing projects, which he thinks will most easily relieve him from his painful embarrassments. He becomes disgusted with the slow and monotonous efforts of the employment to which he was educated, plunges into new plans, and scarcely suspects his danger, till he is irretrievably ruined. Shall I adduce examples?—I forbear.

In the consciousness of owing much which he knows not how to repay, means are suggested, from which conscience at first revolts with abhorrence. But does not the mind turn from these means of relieving its inquietude with less and less aversion, till at length it secretly justifies and adopts them? This indeed is a dreadful consequence of adventuring in debts, beyond our ability of payment; but there is reason to fear that it is not unusual. At least, we have reason to believe, that this state of the mind has a strong tendency to diminish moral susceptibility; and that, however vigorous are his exertions, his virtue is in incessant and the most imminent danger, who has permitted himself to be heavily burdened with a weight of pecuniary obligations.

But why, my brethren, should I attempt to describe the agitations, the sufferings of a man, who either by indiscretion or extravagance, has involved himself in embarrassments, from which he knows not how to extricate himself? It requires no penetration to discern the artifices, by which he is labouring to deceive himself and others; the anguish which preys upon his thoughts, in the apprehension of what he may yet have to experience. Perhaps, to cover the iniquity which must soon be exposed, he involves himself still more deeply; and spreads wider the disappointment and suffering, which the discovery of his guilt will occasion.—To protract the approach of his fall, or with the secret hope of recovering his lost possessions, he flies to the gaming table.—To forget himself, and those whom he has injured, he becomes abandoned to intemperance. His wife and children are the victims of want and sorrow; while he, an outcast from society, and condemned to the gloom of a prison, is perhaps cursed for his perfidy, and covered with disgrace. These are not, indeed, in every instance, the consequences of debts unjustly or imprudently contracted; but to all these evils they certainly expose us; and most impressively does each of them enjoin the apostolick injunction, "owe no man any thing, but to love one another."

A man who contracts a debt, which he has good reason to believe that he shall not be able to pay, or a man who withholds a debt, the justice of which he cannot deny, to the amount of the debt is guilty of deliberate robbery in the sight of God.

It is not a local evil to which the apostle refers in the text, but one which prevails in every society, and which is productive, wherever it prevails, of innumerable calamities. It involves likewise so much vice, that it is surprising that the subject should not obtain the more frequent and solemn consideration of those, who are the professed guardians of publick morals, and whose office it is to persuade men to universal virtue.

This subject, my brethren, has a nearer relation than at first we might imagine, to our interests in the life which awaits us. Of all our transactions in business we must then render an account; and every act of accommodation to the necessitous, every sacrifice which we have made to integrity, will receive its reward; every instance of fidelity in our engagements, from a principle of obedience to the will of God, will be graciously accepted. And then too will every artifice of deceivers be exposed; every mean advantage which they have taken of others, and every act of oppression, which they have done or promoted. Every work of darkness will be brought to light, and every counsel of every heart will be judged. Is not this a subject then of universal, of most solemn interest?

As a brother, I would caution the young religiously to avoid all those projects and indulgences, which, by involving them in debt, will embarrass all their exertions, expose their integrity to innumerable temptations, and render their lives a prey to cares and sorrow. Let the fairness and honesty of the gospel characterize all your dealings; and never hesitate at the loss of any earthly good, which you must part with to retain your uprightness. Let the resolution of holy Job, "till I die, I will not remove my integrity from me," be deliberately and unreservedly adopted. To the upright, there will arise light in the darkness; but the candle of the wicked shall be put out.

Brethren, let us love one another, for love is of God; but while we receive and exercise the accommodation of christians, let us, as far as it is practicable, owe no man anything but love. In all our inter-courses of business, let us feel the presence of *Him* who will call us into judgment and be restrained from every act of injustice. The day is coming, in which the wages of iniquity will be deemed but a miserable compensation for the reproaches of a guilty conscience. In that day may our hearts be gladdened, by the remembrance of temptations successfully resisted, and by His approbation of our virtue, whose favour is eternal life and happiness!

DISCOURSE VI.

MATTHEW v. 44, 45.

Love your enemies, bless them that curse you, do good to them that hate you, and pray for them which despitefully use you, and persecute you ; that ye may be the children of your Father which is in heaven ; ......For HE *maketh His sun to rise on the evil and on the good, and sendeth rain on the just and on the unjust.*

HOW often, my brethren, while pondering upon the instructions of our divine Saviour, does the pious mind repeat the exclamation, "never man spake like this man!" To repress resentment, though it be secretly cherished, is deemed, by men of the world, a considerable attainment in virtue. To forgive offences has been considered the sublime of self-command, and of devotion to duty; and it is an elevation of virtue which few habitually maintain. But Jesus Christ requires far more of all his followers. To be his disciples, we must *love* our enemies; we must *bless* them that curse us, *do good* to them that *hate* us, and *pray* for them that *despitefully use* us, and *persecute* us. Did ever man speak like this man!

Our text exhibits one of the characteristicks of the morality of the gospel; a morality which disdains the smallest accommodation to the prejudices or the vices of the world. It was addressed to men who had been taught to cherish an eternal hatred of all, who did not conform, in every particular, to their own rites and traditions. Israelites who denied the law and the prophets, and Gentiles of every nation, were not considered, by the Jewish doctors, as objects of the command, "thou shalt not kill;" and they justified alike the open and secret murder of heretics whom they could not reclaim. To this exposition of the law, they admitted indeed exceptions;

forbidding the wanton destruction of Gentiles with whom they were not at war, of shepherds who peaceably kept their little flocks, and others of this kind; but at the same time they prohibited a Jew, if he should see one of them falling into the sea, to use any means for his rescue.* Some of these doctors were perhaps among the hearers of the sermon on the mount; and very many who had received their interpretations, as of equal authority with the divine commands. Nay, so much had this hatred of every other people become a national sentiment, that a Roman historian of the first century of the christian æra, when speaking of the Jews, observes, they are faithful towards each other, and ready to exercise the offices of benevolence, but to men of every other country they are the most implacable enemies. These were the men to whom Jesus said, "bless them that curse you, do good to them that hate you, and pray for them that despitefully use and persecute you." It was a precept with

---

*See Lightfoot's Horæ Hebraicæ, Mat. v. 33.

which all their passions and their habits were at war. Yet no attempt is made to reconcile these adverse principles. To be his disciples, to be the children of God, their resentment, and every passion by which it was excited, must be brought into subjection; they must exercise towards all others the forbearance and benevolence, which God was every day exercising towards them. Does not the duty, in this view of it, approve itself to the reason of every ingenuous mind? Observe the beautiful gradation in the command, and the motive by which it is enforced. Love your enemies. Shew that you love them, by returning blessings for curses; by pitying and forgiving them; by addressing them in the language of kindness and of pardon; and pray to God that he may forgive them, that they be preserved as well from the future, as from the present effects of their ungoverned passions. In this resemblance of God, he will recognize you as his children; for he is kind to the evil and to the unthankful. He maketh his sun to rise on the good and on the evil; and sendeth rain on the just and on the unjust.

Our Saviour was not indeed the first who taught the forgiveness of injuries. It was inculcated by the most distinguished philosopher of Greece, four hundred years before the appearance of Christ, and most admirably illustrated by his example.* "To repress resentment is honourable to human nature," says a heathen biographer and moralist.† "But to feel pity for the misfortunes of an enemy, to listen to his supplications, to be ready to relieve him and his children in their embarrassments, discovers a disposition, which he who loves not, has a heart which is black, and fabricated of adamant or iron." The duty has probably been acknowledged by a few of the wise and good of every age of the world; but it had not formed a part of the religious code of any nation, except the Jewish, and by them was so imperfectly understood, and so obscured by idle and

* Socrates.   † Plutarch.   See Grotius upon the text.

selfish expositions, that its very existence could be known only by a recurrence to their laws. But it forms one of the most prominent features in the christian system; and our habitual observance of the duty is one of the conditions, on which we are taught to hope for the mercy of God. From the instructions and the example of Christ, I would therefore define its nature and its extent. This is the object of our discourse; and may God bestow on it his blessing!

The passion of anger forms a part of our moral constitutions, as much as love, or fear, or any other passion; and we have therefore reason to presume that it was intended, like other passions, for good, and not for evil; that it is to be governed, and not destroyed. With this intimation of reason, let us compare the instructions of the gospel; and in this, as in every other instance, we shall find that they are deeply founded in the nature of man.

"If it be possible," says St. Paul, "as much as lieth in you, live peaceably with all men."*   The command implies, if it be not impossible, that it is at least extremely difficult, to live peaceably with some men. Their irritable and obstinate tempers are so easily and so frequently excited, and, though the most unaccommodating of men, they are so unjust in their demands upon others, and are rendered so imperious and cruel by indulgence, that we must not only sacrifice our comfort, but our very virtue, or our lives, if we would maintain tranquillity by the gratification of their humours. With such men, as far as it is possible, in consistency with a conscience void of offence, we are to preserve peace, avoiding as much as we can every cause of provocation; and rather to endure many wrongs than to retaliate. "Hence," says the apostle in the succeeding verse, "dearly beloved, avenge not yourselves, but rather give place unto wrath;" that is, patiently wait for the resentments, the judgments of God; "for it is written, vengeance is mine, I will repay, saith the

* Rom. xii. 19.

Lord." Here it is supposed that indignation of unwarranted injuries may be felt by the best of men; but between this emotion, and the desire of revenge, the distinction is most cautiously preserved. Were it not that anger is naturally and irresistibly excited by great and undeserved indignities or wrongs, the requirement would be without force, and almost without meaning, "if it be possible, as much as lieth in you, live peaceably with all men." But supposing, as it does, not only the existence of the passion, but its very powerful influence, it provides not only against all its excesses, but against the circumstances by which it is excited. If it be impossible to live peaceably with any man, do not unnecessarily exasperate him. Exercise towards him the gentleness and accommodation of the christian temper. But if he will be offended and injure you, though you feel indignant, do not seek satisfaction in revenge. From the evils against which the laws will not defend you, trust your vindication to God. *He* will assert your good name against every calumny; He will repay you for every wrong. This I believe is the spirit of the command; and every well ordered and ingenuous mind will acknowledge its wisdom, and submit to its influence.

"Be ye angry, and sin not; let not the sun go down upon your wrath; neither give place to the devil."*

Here it is supposed that anger may glance into the breast of a wise, a pious man; and where is the man who has not felt it? But to feel the passion is not evil, because it is necessary, and unavoidable. It would be absurd to say, though ye be angry, do not sin, if anger itself, in its first excitement, was sin. The distinction made by the apostle proves, that the passion then only becomes evil, when it is cherished and indulged. Anger, says Solomon, rests, or degenerates into revenge, only in the bosom of fools, or of the wicked. To prevent this degeneracy, the apostle adds, "let not the sun go down upon your wrath,

* Eph. iv. 26, 27.

neither give place to the devil; or to the infernal spirit of resentment." It is a rule admirably adapted to secure us against the dreadful excesses of this passion. Let all the differences of every day be adjusted before the setting of the sun; or at least, before this time, let anger be subjected to the restraints of the will of God, and every thought of retaliation banished from the mind, and the passion would soon become easily reducible to the authority of reason, and of the divine laws. We should not only know, by our own experience, that it is possible to be angry and not to sin, but we should every day be more cautious of giving offence, and better able to bear it. By the knowledge which we should thus acquire of our own hearts, we should constantly be more easily induced to pity and forgive those, who are the victims of a passion which we have learned to controul, and whom we know frequently to suffer more, than with all their malignity they are able to inflict.

"Whosoever shall be angry with his

brother without a cause, shall be in danger of the judgment."*   Here our Lord supposes that there may be a cause which will justify anger.   The question then arises, when is the passion justified?   Before we attempt to answer this inquiry, it is necessary to observe, that it is simply anger, or indignation excited by wrong or injury, to which he alludes, and not resentment; for the gospel does not admit any cause as a justification of revenge.   In what instance then can we justify anger?   Every man supposes, when he feels the passion, that he has cause to feel it.   But the inquiry is too important, it involves too much, to be hastily decided by the opinions of irascible men.   It must be acknowledged too, that in the vast variety of provocations and injuries, by which anger is excited, so much do they often resemble each other, and so blended one with the other are the shades of their guilt, that in our coolest moments, and with all our powers of discrimination, it is not a little difficult to

* Matth. v. 22.

determine precisely, upon christian principles, the boundary which separates justifiable from unlawful anger. St. Mark has mentioned two instances in which the passion was felt by our Lord. And an incident is related by St. John, which obviously implies it. When the Pharisees watched him, to know whether, on the sabbath day, he would heal a man with a withered hand, he looked round about on them *with anger*, being *grieved* for the hardness of their hearts.* He was grieved for *them*, while he was indignant at the *offence* which they had committed. We must admit this distinction, for anger and grief could not, at the same moment, be exercised upon the same object. What then was the offence of the Pharisees? It involved a denial of his divine mission, which he had attested by the most wonderful miracles; and an endeavour, as far as possible, to counteract the purposes for which he came into the world. It was an offence committed against the light, both

* Mark iii. 2—5.

of their own scriptures and of their reasons.
It was the greatest injury which they could
possibly have done, either to others or to
themselves. If any cause can justify
anger, surely it is this. He was indignant
against an offence committed against such
light, such motives, and involving consequences so extensive and awful;—but he
pitied the offenders, instead of pursuing
them with resentment.—Again, says St.
Mark, "they brought young children to
him, that he should touch them; and his
disciples rebuked those who brought them.
But when Jesus saw it, he was much dis-
pleased;" *he was moved with indignation.*
Thus is the expression repeatedly rendered
in the New Testament.* He was indignant at the offence of their resistance; but
he expressed towards them no resentment.
They would have restrained parents from
the attainment of one of the choicest
privileges for their children, the blessing
of their Saviour; a privilege which, thanks
to God, still continues to be the rich

* See Matth. x. 24. and xxvi. 8. and Luke xiii. 14.

inheritance of his church;—and Jesus could not but behold them with much displeasure.—We are informed also by St. John,* that when our Lord went up to Jerusalem, to celebrate the first passover which occurred after his ministry, "he found in the temple those that sold oxen, and sheep, and doves, and the changers of money, sitting." The oxen and doves were sold for the accommodation of those, who could not bring their sacrifices with them; and the money changers, in exchange for other coin, furnished the half shekel, which the law required that every man should offer.† The traffick in itself was lawful; but it was unlawful, it was impious, to pursue it within the limits of the temple, to convert the house of God into a place of merchandise. To have viewed this profanation with indifference was impossible. In Jesus, it excited an irresistible sentiment of abhorrence; and what he strongly felt, he as strongly ex-

* Chap. ii. ver. 13 & seq.
† See Exod. xxx. 13, 15.

pressed. He made a scourge of small cords, and drove them all out of the temple, and the sheep and the oxen; and poured out the changers' money, and overthrew the tables; and said unto them that sold doves, "take these things hence; make not my Father's house a house of merchandize." How strong must have been the indignation, which excited the meek and benevolent Saviour of men to such an act of violence? But it was as distinct from revenge, as it was from approbation. It was not the injury of the *persons* that he designed, but the punishment of the *offence;* an expression of his abhorrence of the profanation of the place, which was consecrated to the worship of God. If then, from the example of Christ, we infer the causes which will justify anger, the number will be comparatively small. The offence must involve important consequences. It must originate in the evil passions of him who commits it; and our indignation must be wholly devoid of selfishness. The gospel does not recognise, in the little disappointments and perplexities of every day, the justification of an irritable and petulant temper; nor does it admit, as a cause of anger, the insults and injuries to which men are exposed, in the common business or intercourses of life. When exposed to such offences, our Lord exhibited no impatience; he uttered no expression of anger. He had no jealousy to be excited; no pride to be mortified; no contracted and selfish feelings to gratify. He did not consider for a moment, to what motives men might attribute his gentleness and forbearance. If the offence involved only his own inconvenience or suffering, his pity, but not his anger, was awakened. If restrained within these limits, anger is not sin. When the laws of God and of man are essentially violated by wanton injustice, we *must* feel indignation, if we love order and virtue; but, like our Lord, we are to attach anger to the *offence*, and not to the *offender*. This is no unwarrantable refinement. It is founded in scripture, and it is practicable; and must necessarily be admitted, if we could reconcile, in any instance, the smallest indulgence of anger, with that forgiveness and love of our enemies, which the gospel demands as a condition of salvation.

But though the gospel supposes that anger may be felt by christians, and that there may be causes which justify it, it utterly forbids retaliation, or revenge. "Ye have heard that it hath been said, an eye for an eye, and a tooth for a tooth." These were punishments which the judges, but not the injured, were permitted to inflict under the Jewish law. It is strictly the law of retaliation; and he who had received injury, had a right to demand its execution. By the same law, a relation of one who was murdered, was allowed with impunity to take the life of the murderer. "But I say unto you," said Jesus, "that ye resist not evil; but whosoever shall smite thee on thy right cheek, turn to him the other also; and if any man will sue thee at the law, and take away thy coat, give him thy cloak also; and whosoever shall compel thee to go a mile, go with him twain." The command, indeed, is not to be interpreted without restrictions, any more than the requirement to hate father and mother, husband and wife, and even our own lives. But it implies, at least, that we should not revenge these indignities and privations. It is parallel with, and best explained by the commands, Be not overcome of evil, but overcome evil with good; and, If thine enemy hunger, feed him; if he thirst, give him drink. It implies that we should rather suffer a repetition of wrongs, than avenge ourselves by a return of violence. With these illustrations in our view, I would endeavour to mark the nature and extent of that forgiveness and love of our enemies, which the gospel inculcates.

Our Lord has defined the nature of forgiveness in our text. The Jews had been taught, not by the law of Moses, but by their own scribes, the appointed teachers of the law, to love their neighbours, or all who were Jews, but to hate their enemies, or all who were Gentiles. This is the sentiment which our Lord particularly opposes in the text. But that he had reference also to the private enmities which they felt towards each other, is evident from the appeal which he immediately added, If ye love those who love you, what reward have you? Do not even the publicans and sinners, whom you hate, the same? And if ye salute your brethren only, do not even the publicans so? What then is the love, the forgiveness, which Jesus demanded? It is, and must be, an affection, which is consistent with indignation at the offence which has been committed. It consists of pity of the disposition in which the evil originated, and a willingness to endure any insults or wrongs rather than to revenge them. It embraces not only a desire of the reformation of the offender, but a readiness to return good for evil, and blessings for curses. It is an affection which will excite us to seek for the injurer the pardon of God. It is a forgiveness as entire, as we hope to receive from God of our own sins. It is the same forbearance and love which God is every day exercising towards the evil and unthankful, continuing to them the blessings which they have forfeited, and by his mercies calling them to repentance. All this is included in the precept, "love your enemies, bless them that curse you, do good to them that hate you, and pray for them who despitefully use you and persecute you, that ye may be the children of your Father who is in heaven; for He maketh His sun to rise on the good and on the evil, and sendeth rain on the just and on the unjust."

From this precept, likewise, might we deduce the *extent* of christian forgiveness. It is adapted to guard every avenue of the heart against the entrance of resentment; to prepare it for every trial, and to secure its successful resistance of every evil passion. But notwithstanding the plainness of this command, the means which it prescribes of obeying it, and the motives by which it is enforced; notwithstanding the frequency, and the varied manner of its repetition, even the apostles did not fully comprehend its meaning. How often, said Peter, shall my brother sin against me, and I forgive him? Till seven times? Suppose the inquiry had been proposed to a Roman philosopher; to him who is admitted to have been the wisest and the best man, as well as the most consummate orator which Rome ever produced. What would have been his answer? It is written in his familiar letters to his friends. "I hate the man, said he, and will hate him, and wish that I could be revenged." "I would revenge every crime according to the degree of its provocation."* Suppose it to have been proposed to a Jewish teacher. We have his answer in the decrees of their doctors. "Three offences are to be forgiven, but not the fourth." But what was the reply of Jesus? Observe it, my brethren; and remark in it the extent of that forgiveness which he requires us to exercise. "Shall I forgive my brother seven

---

*Grotius de verit. relig. christ. lib. 2. 12.

times?" Without doubt Peter proposed this inquiry, with a full conviction that it would obtain the admiration and applause of Jesus; and it probably implied a benevolence, of which he had never formed any conception, till he had become a follower of Christ. "Shall I forgive my brother seven times?" "I say not unto thee," said Jesus, "until seven times; but until seventy times seven." Thou shalt forgive as frequently as provocations are renewed. Thou shalt never revenge. "Shouldst not thou have compassion on thy fellow servant, even as thy Lord had pity on thee? If thou hopest that God will forgive thee thy debt of ten thousand talents, shouldst not thou forgive thy fellow servant, who owest thee an hundred pence?" The precept is perfect. It admits of no additions and no exceptions. Let us view its illustration in the example of Christ.

We have adverted to the tenderness, *the grief* which our Lord exhibited towards those, who were watching whether he would heal on the sabbath day, that they

might accuse him. It was in his mind a
sentiment far stronger, than the indignation which their conduct excited; for of
this we have no evidence in any expression
which he uttered. His language was the
most dispassionate, the most worthy of his
character. " Is it lawful," said he, "to do
good on the sabbath day, or to do evil; to
save life or to kill?" By the same class
of men he was perpetually followed with
the most insidious designs; at one time
proposing inquiries, the answers to which,
they imagined, must necessarily expose
him to the judgments, either of the civil
or the ecclesiastical authorities; and at
another, attributing the most beneficent
exertions to infernal agency. But, instead
of repulsing them with angry revilings, he
never failed to resolve the doubts which
they suggested, and to renew in their
presence those evidences of his divine
mission, which were adapted to produce
conviction, and grateful acknowledgment.
How admirably did this conduct illustrate
and enforce the requirement, "do good to

23

them that hate you?" He denounced indeed the most awful judgments against the scribes and pharisees. He called them hypocrites; he compared them to whited sepulchres, and to graves which appear not. But he applied every means of bringing them to repentance. He practised towards them all the forgiveness and the affection which he inculcated. Under the most accumulated insults and injuries, his forbearance was perfect. We discover no feeling, but of compassion for his enemies. We hear no expression, which is not adapted to convert their wrath into penitential sorrow, the warmest love, and the most entire devotion to his service. His pity for their blindness, their obduracy, and his zeal for their reformation, were greater even than their own vengeance. He did not cease, even to the last moment of life, to seek for them the compassion, the pardon of God. This is christian forgiveness. It is to pity the offender, while we are indignant at the offence. It is to return for the curses of those who would

injure us, prayers to God for their pardon
and reformation; and every benevolent
effort which their circumstances may require, for the malignant purposes which
they have formed, or have accomplished
against us. It is to be merciful to them,
as God is merciful to us. It is to forgive,
as we hope to be forgiven. All this is
comprehended in that love of our enemies
which the gospel inculcates. All this is
taught as clearly, and far more impressively,
in the example, as in the precepts of Christ.

Let this mind then be in us, which was
also in our divine Teacher and Saviour.
Let us learn of him, when reviled, never
to revile again, and when suffering, never
to threaten revenge. With the anger
which is excited by an offence, let us feel
grief for the unhappy offender. Let us
pity his disposition, be admonished against
its indulgence, and be ready to exercise
towards him every office of christian benevolence. That no desire of retaliation,
that no sentiment of revenge may rankle
in our hearts, let us seek for him the

pardon and blessing of God. This is one of the conditions on which we are taught to hope for the forgiveness of our own sins. May God enable us to comply with it! Putting away wrath and clamour, and evil speaking, be ye kindly affectioned one towards another, forbearing and forgiving, even as ye hope that God, for Christ's sake, will forgive us. To Him be glory forever. AMEN!

I was in the spirit on the Lord's day.

An acknowledgment of the being and government of God, and of the dependence and obligations of man, involves the duty of expressing to our Creator and Benefactor the homage of our adoration, our gratitude, and our submission. The obligation to worship God is indeed as obvious from the deductions of reason, as from the requirements of revelation ; and he is as irrational, as he is impious, by whom the duty is denied, or wantonly violated.

It cannot, however, have escaped the notice of any, who are familiar with the scriptures, how important the institution of the sabbath was regarded by God, and with what frequency and solemnity the command to observe it was repeated, under each of the ancient dispensations. On a subject so interesting, man was not left to the guidance of reason alone. Even in paradise, where he was admitted to the most intimate communion with God, and where we may suppose that a considerable portion of every day was appropriated to the offices of devotion; in paradise, where man was restricted only by one prohibition, and before his understanding had become perverted, and his affections depraved, God required the consecration of the sabbath peculiarly to his service. When he rested on the seventh day of the world, he blessed, and sanctified it. Under every economy, it was, perhaps, the most effectual barrier against the idolatry and vice, by which his people was surrounded; and if every encroachment upon it had been early and resolutely resisted, they would have escaped innumerable judgments. The

sabbath was constantly and reverently observed by our Lord; and though the day
was changed from the seventh, to the first
of the week, in memory of his resurrection,
his faithful disciples, in every succeeding
age, have imitated his example, and devoted a seventh portion of their time, to
the peculiar duties and offices of religion.
I cannot suppose that this change was
made by the apostles, unauthorized by
their Master. Many and important communications were made to them after his
resurrection; and I am persuaded, that
the observance of this day as a sabbath,
was then appointed by Christ. With all
their zeal and boldness, they would not
have dared to make this change, without
an express command. Being the day in
which he rose from the dead, it was called
the Lord's day, the sabbath of christians.
The sabbath of the Jews was instituted to
commemorate the completion of the creation of the world. The christian sabbath
commemorates an event infinitely more
interesting, the resurrection of the Author

of our faith. It is the day in which Christ triumphed over death. How appropriate, then, is the designation! With what pious gratitude should we hail this day, and with what fidelity consecrate it to the worship of God!

"I was in the spirit," says St. John, "on the Lord's day." The expression, "in the spirit," refers to that state of the mind, which is produced by the reception of any extraordinary divine influence. It is synonymous with the expression of St. Luke concerning Peter, "he fell into a trance;" and perhaps with what Paul says of himself, that he "was caught up into the third heavens." When "in the spirit," he received the revelations, which contain the history of the church to its latest ages; and these revelations were made to him "on the Lord's day." It is with reference only to the name of the day, that I have selected the text; and I could avail myself of it, to shew our obligations to its observance; the objects to which it should be appropriated; the benefits of which it may

be productive ; and the causes and consequences of its neglect. These are subjects
of sufficient interest and importance to
demand attention.

1. We should observe this day, because
it was *for us* that Christ taught, and suffered, and died, and rose from the dead.
We are bound to its observance by motives
as numerous, as our obligations to the
Saviour. And can you number, can you
repay these obligations? I refer you only
to some of the most prominent, as excitements to keep holy this day of the Lord.
To Christ we are indebted for our
knowledge of God. The world by its own
wisdom, never knew God. Before the
christian era, he was worshipped by no
nation, except the Jews. In ages and
countries the most polished and learned,
scarcely less ignorance prevailed of God
and of his worship, than in the most unenlightened times, and the most barbarous
state of society. In the most refined city
of heathen antiquity, the most distinguished philosopher and best citizen was

condemned to suffer death, because he taught the existence of one God. Without a revelation, without the gospel, we might at this moment have been in equal ignorance and depravity. Here then is a motive to the observance of this day; for we celebrate *his* resurrection, who has taught us what God is, and what is the service which he requires of his rational family.—To Christ we are also indebted for our knowledge of *the will* of God. I do not say that all the laws of the gospel were unknown, till they were promulgated by the Saviour; but the gospel itself furnishes abundant evidence, how confused and inadequate were the sentiments of virtue which prevailed both among Jews and heathens, at the time of the appearing of Christ. He separated truth from the errour with which it was mingled, taught it in its perfect purity, and enforced it at once by the most interesting and awful motives, which were ever proposed to influence the conduct of man. By all the benefits and pleasures which result from our knowledge of the divine will, we are therefore bound to celebrate the day of the resurrection of our Lord.—From him likewise have we derived the assurance, that sin may be forgiven, and that God will admit the penitent offender to all the honours and happiness of his kingdom. He came to bind up the broken hearted, to preach deliverance to the captives, and and to die the just for the unjust. We can obtain assurance of the forgiveness of sins, only from the gospel: It is offered to repenting sinners, only through faith in the blood of Christ. By rising from the dead, he demonstrated the efficacy of his cross. And should we not therefore keep holy the day, distinguished by a triumph so glorious? If we are sensible of the guilt of our sins, and feel the repentance which Jesus requires, every faculty of our souls will be engaged, on this day, in rendering to God the homage which he claims. It is through Christ also that we have access to God in prayer; and to him we are indebted for the confidence, with which we may approach the throne of the Almighty; for the consolation, strength, and joy, of which this holy intercourse is productive. We are taught to ask for every blessing in his name; to hope for every spiritual good, through the influence of the grace which he has brought to the world. What day, then, can be so interesting to christians, as that of the resurrection of their Lord? What institution is enforced by more powerful motives?

2. We should observe the christian sabbath, because it is at once an emblem of heaven, and a means of its attainment. Engaged as we are through the week in the toils of business, and the pursuit of pleasure, and experiencing all the cares, and the alternate elevations and depressions of success and of misfortune, what would be the condition of society, if there was no season of repose, and of serious reflection? On this day we are called to consider, that this world is not our home; that we were created for employments and for gratifications infinitely higher than

those to which we are excited by our senses; that we are accountable for all our advantages and our conduct; and that our condition in eternity will depend on the tastes, the affections, and the habits, which we form in this world. In the employments of this day, does the faithful disciple of Christ find his principles of piety and virtue to acquire new strength, his hopes to be raised, his erroneous sentiments corrected, and his heart and his life made better. In these employments, and in the anticipations which they awaken, he finds that peace which the world cannot give him; he feels his capacity of immortal happiness, in the presence of his Redeemer and his God. And are not these sources of obligation to the observance of this day? If we are christians, we shall feel these effects of the sabbath; and if we feel them, we shall acknowledge the duty of hallowing the day peculiarly to the service of God.

But what are the objects to which this

day should be appropriated? I will endeavour to answer this inquiry.

1. As the sabbath which we observe,
in compliance with the original appointment of God, consists of a seventh part of
time, it should be devoted to purposes
consistent with the design of God, in
blessing and sanctifying the seventh day.
Most men, during the business of the
week, find but little time for self-examina-
tion, for the study of the scriptures, and
for private devotion; or if they have
leisure, claim it for indulgence in the
amusements of the world. On the sabbath, these duties should obtain peculiar
attention. We should inquire what we
have been doing; what are the principles
and motives by which we have been actuated; what are our propensities and desires; what we have omitted which we
ought to have done; what is the account
which we must render of the past, and
what are our duties for the future? It is
designed to be a day of rest from the
ordinary pursuits of life, but not a day of

indolence. To commune, as we ought, with our hearts; to study the word of God with the reverence and attention which it claims, and in secret to confess our sins; to seek the divine guidance, to cherish the gratitude and love which we owe to God, and to commit ourselves and our concerns to his care, furnish abundant occupation for all the hours of this day, which may be spared from its other duties. It was a command of God to the Jews, "from evening to evening shall ye celebrate your sabbath;"* and greatly would it conduce to a suitable observance of the day, if our sabbaths were always commenced on the evening of Saturday. It would predispose us to meet the day with the interest and the dispositions which it should awaken, by divesting our minds of the calculations and inquietudes of the week. It would make these employments sources to us of the highest improvement, and the purest pleasure.

2. We should hallow this day in our

* Lev. xxiii. 32.

houses, by the exercises of domestick worship. Every father should be a priest in
his house. Every house should be a
temple of the living God, from which the
incense of prayer should daily ascend to
heaven. But on the sabbath, there should
be peculiar and distinguishing offices of
domestick piety. We should shew to our
families the reverence which we feel for
the day, by preventing, as far as possible,
all domestick labours; by dispensing to
them instruction, and enforcing it by our
examples. Let each fill the little sphere
of his own house, by the faithful discharge
of its duties, and blessings of incalculable
worth will result to society. With what
increased zeal and pleasure will the devout
heart engage in the *publick* worship of
God, which has kindled the holy flame, by
the exercises of social worship at home?
They prepare us to recognize our relation
to the family of man, and to commend all
to the favour of our common Father. They
have the best influence in qualifying the
mind for that reception of truth, by which

its effects will be rendered permanent and happy.

3. In giving us rest from the common business of life, the sabbath furnishes to parents a most favourable season for the religious instruction of their children. On this day they meet, with every advantage, for communicating and receiving knowledge; and it is our solemn duty to avail ourselves of this time, to induce them to that piety and virtue, on which depend the happiness of this, and of the future life; to teach them that there is a God of perfect power, benevolence, and holiness; that he is always present with us; that all things are subject to his providence, and that he will call all men into judgment. That he loves truth, and hates iniquity; that he sent Jesus to be the instructor of the ignorant, and the Saviour of sinners; that he will always hear our prayers, when they are offered with sincere hearts; and that he is more willing to do us good, than we are to ask for it. We should warn them of the deceitfulness of the world, and

of their own hearts, and of the necessity of constant watchfulness. We should allure them to a love of holiness, by exhibiting the joys of heaven; and deter them from vice, by representing its terrible consequences in hell. These instructions are suited to the comprehensions of children at a very early age. At least, they may be sufficiently understood, to obtain a powerful and most beneficial influence on their conduct. They are truths which the sabbath is adapted to bring to our recollections with peculiar force, and which pious parents will not fail of inculcating on their offspring. How delightful a spectacle is the domestick circle, in which children surround their parents, listening with eagerness and delight to the lessons of wisdom, which are inculcated from the word of God! Let them see in our prayers, in the books which we read, and in our pious conversation, the genuine influence of religion, and they will catch the spirit with which we are actuated, and learn of us to glorify our and their Father in heaven.

4. It was the practice of the primitive church, to assemble on this day for the publick worship of God, and to observe the ordinance of the supper. The communion was then a part of the service of every sabbath, and every one, who acknowledged the divine mission of Christ, was a communicant. The disciples met, not in churches erected for their worship, but in each other's houses; and in assembling, were often obliged to observe the greatest secrecy, that they might avoid the interruption and persecutions of their enemies. Yet were these most happy sabbaths; for it was then deemed by christians one of the best of their privileges, to unite in the worship of God, and to hear the doctrines and duties of his word illustrated and enforced. It was, I apprehend, peculiarly with reference to the benefits which would result from publick worship, that the sabbath was instituted; but in instituting the publick

exposition of the scriptures on this day, as a part of the duties of the ministers of his religion, has the interest and importance of social worship been vastly augmented. "Discourses to the people on the nature of their duties to their Maker, their fellow mortals, and themselves, was an idea too august to be mingled with the absurd and ridiculous, or profligate and barbarous rites of paganism";* And although the scriptures were read in the synagogues of the Jews, discourses, like those of the apostles, were wholly unknown. "It is an institution for which mankind are indebted to christianity; introduced by the Founder himself of this divine religion, and in every point of view worthy of its high original. Its effects have been to soften the tempers, and to purify the morals of mankind; not in so high a degree as benevolence could wish, but enough to call forth the warmest strains of our gratitude." It has been one

* Adams's introductory oration on rhetorick and oratory, pp. 23, 4.

of the most efficient means, I believe that I may say that it has been the most effectual of all the means which have been employed, to extend to every class of society the most important knowledge. It has the happiest tendency to the restraint of vice, and to the encouragement of piety and virtue. To these publick services, therefore, should a portion of the day be devoted; and they will be conscientiously and devoutly observed by every one, who is interested to promote the best good of society, and who estimates, as he ought, the importance of the privilege.

5. St. Paul directed the Corinthian christians, on the first day of the week, to lay by them in store, as God had prospered them, that they might contribute to the necessities of their poor and persecuted brethren. Offices of charity are appropriate to all times; and they are considered as of so much importance in the christian system, that they must be performed, even though they interfere with

the other duties of the sabbath. To visit the sick and the afflicted, to administer to them the consolations and encouragements of the gospel, and if they are in want, to relieve them, not only encourages in *them* pious sentiments and affections, but is productive of the same important effects in ourselves. One of the earliest writers of the christian church, says, "the citizens assemble on the sabbath, and first are read the scriptures of the prophets and the apostles. The priest then delivers a discourse, in which he exhorts the people to practise what they have heard. Then all join in prayer, after which the ordinance of the supper is administered, and then they give alms to the poor. This is the manner of conducting the christian festival." * Difference of times, and of the circumstances of christians, have brought these contributions into disuse, as one of the peculiar duties of the sabbath; but as we have opportunity, we should on this day

* Justin Martyr, Apol. 2, in Taylor's Ductor Dubitantium, p. 364.

dispense to the necessities of others ; and particularly cherish the benevolent dispositions, which will impel us, when occasions offer, to do good unto all.

Even by the politician, whose views are confined to the order, the improvement and the comfort of society in this world, the sabbath is considered as one of the wisest and most beneficial institutions which was ever devised. By its slow and silent operation, it allays the ferment of those evil passions, which are excited by the sordid, the selfish, and the sensual pursuits of mankind ; and even where it is much neglected, it produces a moral influence more favourable to human happiness, than could be derived from any laws or appointments, unaccompanied by a divine sanction. To the weekly sabbath are we greatly indebted for the tranquillity and security in which we live ; for much of the efficacy of those sentiments, principles and affections, which are the strongest cement of the social compact. If it were universally observed as a divine institution, it would relieve society of many of its most oppressive burdens, supersede the necessity of many laws, and be one of the best means of promoting confidence and of diffusing happiness through all the classes of society, and the relations of life.

To the poor, the sabbath is adapted to be an inestimable blessing. It is a peculiarity of the gospel, that it addresses itself equally to the poor and to the unknown, as to the affluent and the honoured. "Go and tell John," said our Lord to those who came to him to inquire if he were the Messiah, "Go and tell John, that the poor have the gospel preached to them." This he addressed to the baptist, as an evidence of his divine mission; as an evidence that he came from Him who is the common Father of man, and who regardeth not the rich more than the poor. In the very beginning of his ministry he proclaimed at Nazareth, that it was one of the purposes of his mission, to preach the gospel to the poor; to enlighten and to comfort that large portion of society, which had been despised and disregarded. " Poverty was considered by the Jews as a punishment from God;"* and notwithstanding the numerous requirements of their law to the exercise of benevolence, "Amos reproaches the Israelites, with having sold the poor for a contemptible price, as for shoes and sandals."* But, neglected as they were, the poor of Judea were the most privileged of the world; for to them, every seventh day was a day of rest. It was the interest of their teachers to retain them in ignorance, that they might themselves retain their authority. But Jesus made them the objects of his peculiar care ; and under his, and the ministry of the apostles, they were instructed in all the doctrines and duties of religion, and excited to piety and virtue by the most interesting, consolatory, and powerful motives. In every other part of the civilized world, the condition of the poor was inconceivably more deplorable. They were immersed in the deepest

---

*Calmet's Dict. art. Poor and Poverty.

ignorance, as a means of retaining them as instruments for accomplishing the designs of ambition, of avarice, or of pride. The fame of the refinement and learning of antiquity is derived, not from a wide diffusion of knowledge over society, but from the genius and acquirements of a few, who appear, in comparison, as a different race of beings. The poor were the slaves of the most debasing superstition; and the very rites of their religion, instead of enlightening, involved them in still deeper darkness; and in some instances were adapted to promote their progress in vice and wretchedness. The doctrines of philosophy were taught to the rich, to the powerful, and to men who were capable, by their talents, of commanding influence in society; but the design of raising the poor from their depressed condition, by diffusing knowledge among them, and by inculcating principles and motives adapted to secure their virtue, never entered the minds of their most distinguished sages; or if for a moment suggested, was deemed an enterprise too bold to be attempted. It was left for the son of God to rescue this vast portion of mankind from their degradation and misery; and one of the most important means of effecting this most benevolent, this sublime object, was the institution of the services of the sabbath. Under the christian dispensation, the poorest and most ignorant of the Gentile world were invited to receive the same instructions, which were dispensed to the rich and the learned. They were taught to appropriate a seventh portion of their time exclusively to the attainment of a knowledge of the gospel.

They were instructed that, equally as their superiours, they were the children of God, accountable for their conduct, and capable of attaining immortal happiness. Where christianity is unknown, the condition of the poor is at this day the most distressing which can be imagined; and even in christian countries their sufferings are augmented, in proportion to their neglect of the institution of the sabbath.

Considering then this single effect of the observance of this day, is it not worthy of divine appointment, and of our warmest gratitude? May I not say, wherever the benign influence of the gospel has extended, that it has doubled the number of rational beings, by restoring to half of mankind the reason they had lost, and the rank and privileges to which they are entitled, as accountable and immortal beings? Without the gospel, without the opportunities and services of this day, many of us would have been, at this moment, in the lowest mental and moral debasement; and shall we not then keep holy to God the season to which we are so essentially indebted for our most valuable blessings?

2. A proper observance of the sabbath is adapted to have the happiest influence on domestick life. The business of the world separates men from their families; absorbs, for most of every day, their cares and affections; and has a direct tendency to excite and to cherish the social and un-

social passions of avarice, of envy, and jealousy. On the sabbath, the common labours of life are suspended, and leisure is allowed for a day at home. On this day, unincumbered by other cares, may fathers and mothers unite their exertions in the cultivation of the minds and hearts of their children; and by exercising together the offices of piety, elevate, and strengthen, and refine the flame of their affection. The family, in which, for six days of the week, the cares and passions of the world have been indulged, in the sabbath may find a season of peace; a few hours for undisturbed meditation; for secret and for social prayer; for a review of life, and for the indulgence of plans and hopes, the objects of which are far without the limits of this life. Conceive of a family, on the evening preceding the sabbath, retiring from their labours, divesting their minds of the calculations and inquietudes of the world, and assembling in the full exercise of the pious and benevolent affections, which the gospel inculcates. How well adapted are all their intercourses and employments, to the security of the best happiness of man ! On this day the dispositions are corrected, in which originate the contentions and miseries of domestick life. All the amiable and endearing qualities of the temper are cherished, and the principles and habits which give energy and worth to the character, are strengthened. To the influence of the christian sabbath are we much indebted for the delightful associations, which we attach to the idea of home ; for the virtues which peculiarly constitute the happiness of domestick life. Faithfully discharge its duties, my brethren, and you will find it one of the most effectual means of promoting union, order, and affection in your houses ; of exciting in your children sentiments of piety and virtue ; and of securing to you, in your own homes, a refuge from the disappointments, the perplexities, and the vices of the world.

3. It is an immediate effect of the sabbath to harmonize the discordant materials of which society is composed. It

brings together many, who could never have been united from inclination, and awakens in their breasts a mutual interest. We meet on this day, not to indulge our selfish views and pursuits, but to rejoice in each other's welfare, and to sympathize in each other's sufferings. We meet, not as men of business, whose plans are liable to interference, and in whom a similarity of occupations and views awakens suspicion and distrust; but as the children of the same Father, seeking an interest in the grace which is abundant for all; and whose success, instead of being retarded, will be most essentially advanced, by all the assistance which we can render to each other. To this cause, perhaps, more than to any other, are we to attribute, that sensibility to the wants of others, and those enlarged principles of benevolence, which distinguish modern from ancient times, and christian countries from those, which are unenlightened by revelation. The spirit of the gospel is love; and the disciples of Christ meet on this day to worship that Being, who is essential love. They meet as brethren. In this relation the rich and the poor, the wise and the ignorant, the honoured and the despised, stand together before God. They meet to humble themselves together before *Him*, who is no respecter of persons ; they acknowledge together their sins, their dependence, and their wants. Could any other means be devised, so well adapted to excite in man a widely extended sympathy, to animate him in the discharge of every relative duty, and to secure to him the most permanent possession of every social pleasure.

4. To the sabbath are we much indebted for our knowledge of the principles of religion, and for their efficacy upon our conduct. Very many of those who are best acquainted with the gospel, will not hesitate to avow their obligations, for the leisure which this day affords to them, and for the excitements which they have received in the house of God, to the study of his word. In the multiplicity and variety of our ordinary pursuits, how rarely

do we find, that we have time or inclination to think seriously of God, of our duties, of heaven and of judgment? It may even be questioned, if the sabbath were abolished, whether nine-tenths of the christian world, after two or three generations, would not become wholly ignorant or regardless of moral truth. It is to the secret, but most salutary influence of this day, that we are to attribute much of the virtue on which we are accustomed to rely, in our inter-courses with mankind. It is a season in which, if we have any sensibility, we shall feel repentance, and form pious resolutions. Once in the week at least, it pre-pares us to go into the world, in some measure disposed and enabled to resist its temptations.—Once in the week, at least, do thousands hear the scriptures, to whose minds they would otherwise have no ac-cess; and they are arrested by rebukes, by warnings or encouragements, which force them to feel, that they were not created only for this world. To those who are disposed wisely to improve it, it is a season most favourable to accessions of religious knowledge, and to the advancement of habits of piety and virtue; and I believe that I may appeal to the experience of many to confirm the assertion, that in its proper observance is one of the best securities of the order, the success, and the pleasures of the week.

But why should I attempt to enumerate the benefits of the christian sabbath? No conception of its importance can be formed by those who do not observe it; and they who keep it holy to the Lord, derive from it advantages and gratifications, which cannot be expressed. To them, it is a refuge from the storms of the world; a shadow from its oppressive heat. They hail its arrival; they enjoy every moment of its progress; and derive from its duties a cheerfulness and elevation, which results from none of the common pursuits and indulgences of life. It is an emblem of the rest of heaven. If we hallow it in our hearts, in our houses, and in the church; if we faithfully appropriate it to its proper

services, these will be its effects; and by
these influences shall we have conviction,
that its services are acceptable to God.

That this day is greatly disregarded,
both in the domestick and publick duties
which it involves, is one of the most
obvious of the facts which arrests our
notice, in a moral survey of society. The
causes and consequences of this neglect
demand our attention; for in proportion
as it can be obviated, we aid in staying
the current of vice and misery, and in promoting the virtue and best happiness of
man. With all the seriousness which the
subject claims, I propose then the inquiry,
why are the privileges of this day so little
estimated, and its most important duties
so frequently violated?

The cause, my brethren, which is the
most obvious, of the neglect of the obligations of the sabbath, is an excessive love
of the world, and an inordinate devotion
to its interests. For six days, in succes-
sion, we are permitted to labour; and to
accumulate, as far as we may by honest

industry, the riches of the world.—During this time, little relaxation is allowed from the ardour of pursuit. We commence our toils. Care immediately presses upon care, and calculation succeeds to calculation. Every hour is deemed important, and is most faithfully appropriated to the objects of our affections and our hopes. We close the day, exhausted with its labours; and full of the anticipation of purposes yet to be accomplished, we seek the refreshment of sleep. In the morning, when we are best prepared for the exercises of devotion, the mind is so much absorbed by its anticipations and its plans, that the obligations of piety are wholly forgotten; and the mind which, through the day, has not been raised above the earth, and which sympathises with the fatigue and enervation of the body, will not be disposed, at evening to engage in those exercises, which force us to a comparison of our conduct with our duties and of the riches of this world with the treasures of heaven. In this condition, the sabbath overtakes us; and we welcome it, perhaps, as a day of rest. But though actual labour is suspended, the thoughts and affections flow on in their accustomed channels, nor can they easily be diverted from their course. Hence it is that many waste the morning of this day in sleep; that the religious instruction of children, for which this time furnishes an opportunity the most favourable, is so much neglected; and the publick worship of God is treated with so much indifference. Hence it is that the conversation of men on the sabbath is confined, almost as exclusively to the business of the world, as if this were the purpose for which we assembled. My brethren, these things ought not so to be. A few moments of every morning and evening, devoted to secret and to domestick prayer, and an hour occasionally given to the reading of the scriptures, and to familiar conversation on religious subjects, would occasion no material deduction, even from the pecuniary profits of a day, nor would they interfere with any rational pleasure; and they would prepare us to meet the sabbath as a day to be consecrated to God, and conducive at once to the greatest benefits, and the richest enjoyment. We cannot, at the same time, serve God and Mammon; and if all our thoughts and our solicitude through the week are confined to the possessions and pleasures of this world, the sabbath will be a day of weariness and of pain, which we shall be easily induced to squander in indolence, or to profane in vice. There is indeed no necessary interference between the ordinary business of life, and the duties of religion; but to derive pleasure or advantage from the service of God, we must love him supremely; and if we thus love him, we shall be ready to make any sacrifices for the enjoyment of his service. We shall permit no care or pursuit to prevent our observance of his requirements. We shall shew forth his loving kindness every morning, and his faithfulness every night; and hallow his sabbath as a pledge of the rest which remains for his people in heaven.

But the cause to which the neglect of this day is principally to be attributed, is the want of religion in our hearts; our insensibility of the obligations which we owe to Christ, whose triumph over death we this day celebrate; our inconsideration of our sins, of the authority of his commands, the worth of his promises, and the terror of his denunciations. If we feel the repentance, the gratitude, the love of God and of man which his gospel inculcates, the hunger and thirst for increasing righteousness which it is adapted to excite, and the spirit of devotion which it awakens in its sincere believers; if we were interested to know and to perform the will of God, as we are interested in the pleasures and business of the world, no duty of the day would be wantonly disregarded. It is to this inconsideration, this insensibility of the power and excellence of religion, that we are to attribute the dominion of those sensual and selfish passions, which attach us to the world, and indispose us to the offices of piety. I do not say that an observance of the publick services of the sabbath is a certain evidence of piety in the heart; but I believe that it will be difficult to find exceptions to the remark, that they who disregard the publick worship of this day, are equally regardless of religion in their families, and inattentive to its requirements in their own lives. We do not therefore form our judgments precipitately, nor violate the law of charity, when we accuse him of practical infidelity, and of a heart which resists the impressions of divine truth, who easily excuses the neglect of the duties of this day, or observes its publick rites with thoughtless indifference. To this insensibility, this want of religion in the heart, are all the other causes of the neglect of the sabbath to be ascribed; and the evil can be remedied by no other means, than the purification of the source in which it originates. When we feel the genuine influence of religion, no persuasions will be necessary to bring us to the house of God. If we love Him who died, and rose, and lives to save us, we shall keep holy the day of his resurrection. The effect is inseparable from the cause. If we love Christ, we shall be excited by our love to habitual exertions to keep all his commandments.

The consequences of the neglect of the sabbath are most solemn and affecting, nor does it require much penetration to discern them. Would to God that a recurrence to them might admonish us of our dangers.

The first effect which we notice, is an increasing disregard of moral and religious restraints. A man does not wantonly neglect the sabbath, till he has become insensible, to a considerable degree, of the influence of religious principles ; and when, in consequence of this insensibility, he disregards the services of this day, his progress in evil will be daily accelerated. Every one who has ever improved this day to the purposes for which it was instituted, has occasionally at least felt its restraints in the conduct of the week. The principles which were then impressed on his mind have recurred with so much force,

that he has been strengthened to successful resistance, where he would otherwise
have been overcome, and to greater fidelity
in the discharge of every duty.   But when
we have learned to dispense with one
acknowledged obligation, every other is
violated with greater ease; for we cannot
habitually violate one, till we have lost that
reverence of the authority of God, which
is the only security of virtue.   When we
have ceased to feel any interest in the
worship of God, we shall derive no pleas-
urable emotions from a remembrance of his
presence, and of his commands; we shall
feel no disposition to refer to our account-
ability, and to the sanctions of his law. Of
this consequence of a violation of the
sabbath, there are many examples; and
they exhibit to the young most solemn
warnings, against a practice, which is
fraught with so much evil. It increases
the hardness of the heart, emboldens to
the commission of vice, and separates us
farther from God. From a wanton neglect
of this day, to a profanation of it, and from

a profanation of it to a rejection of every religious restraint, the transition is so easy, that we may generally venture to predict of him, in whom the return of the sabbath awakens no religious sentiments, and who feels no remorse in appropriating it to the pursuits of business, or of worldly pleasure, that he is not far from the lowest state of moral debasement; a condition of ultimate, and unutterable misery.

The abuse of the sabbath has a direct tendency to promote domestick disunion and wretchedness. In their private and family worship, in their study of the word of God, in their religious education of their children, and in the publick services of the day, do the pious experience a sweet serenity of mind, most delightful exercises of their understandings and affections, and the most earnest desires to love God more, and to serve him better. The evil dispositions and passions in which this abuse originates, are in themselves sources of misery. In the families in which the sabbath is neglected and profaned, low and selfish and sordid motives obtain ascendancy; and every contrariety of feeling, every difference of opinion, every trivial disappointment, produces petulance, and perhaps contention; and where there is domestick contention, there is confusion and every evil work.

3. The profanation of the sabbath is peculiarly fatal in its influence on the minds and conduct of children. Reared from their infancy in the disregard of the word and ordinances of God, their hearts acquire an obduracy, which resists all the impressions of religion. In the dying confessions of those, whose lives have been forfeited by the laws of society, their early habits of vice have been attributed, principally, to an early neglect and abuse of the sabbath. What an affecting admonition is this to all who are parents? By permitting our children to grow vile, without imposing on them the restraints, and exciting them by the encouragements of religion, we become instrumental of their abandonment to evil, and of their final

misery. Thousands, who might have been the ornaments and blessings of society, by parental neglect have become lost to virtue, and the bane of their generation ; have passed a corrupted and a miserable existence, and have died without accomplishing one purpose of their being.

Let these consequences of its abuse operate as motives to keep holy this day of the Lord. A time will arrive, when we must account for the use which we have made of all our opportunities of religious instruction. May God enable us so to improve these seasons, that we may render our account of them with joy! There remaineth a rest, an eternal sabbath, for the people of God. Happy, infinitely happy are they, who are admitted to its employments and its joys. May God make them our happy portion, through Jesus Christ, to whom be glory forever. AMEN.

FINIS.

List of the Members

OF

"THE SOCIETY FOR PROMOTING CHRISTIAN KNOWLEDGE, PIETY, AND CHARITY,"

By whom the Christian Monitor is published.

MAY, 1811.

John L. Abbot, A. M.	Cambridge.
Rev. Isaac Allen,	Bolton.
Joseph Allen, esq.	Worcester.
Mr. Samuel Allen,	do.
Rev. John Allyn,	Duxboro'.
Rev. John Andrews,	Newburyport.
Rev. Aaron Bancroft, D. D.	Worcester.
Rev. Thomas Barnard, D. D.	Salem.
Mr. Edward Blake,	Boston.
Rev. John Bradford,	Roxbury.
Alden Bradford, esq.	Wiscasset.
Samuel Bradford, esq.	Boston.
Mr. Andrew Brimmer,	do.
Rev. Joseph S. Buckminster,	do.
John Callender, esq.	do.
Rev. Samuel Cary,	do.
Mr. Samuel Chandler,	Worcester.
Elisha Clap, A. M.	Boston.
Rev. Pitt Clark,	Norton.
Rev. Samuel Clark,	Burlington, Ver.
Rev. Henry Colman,	Hingham.
Mr. Joseph Coolidge, jun.	Boston.
Rev. Henry Cumings, D. D.	Billerica.
Mr. Josiah Davis,	Concord.
Rev. John Eliot, D. D.	Boston.
* Rev. William Emerson,	do.
Hon. Oliver Fiske,	Worcester.
Rev. John Fiske,	Newbraintree.
Rev. Jacob Flint,	Cohasset.
Rev. Edmund Foster,	Littleton.

Rev. John Foster,   Brighton.
Rev. Joel Foster,   Sudbury.
Mr. David Francis,   Boston.
His Honour William Gray,   do.
Rev. Thomas Gray,   Roxbury
Rev. Thaddeus M. Harris,   Dorchester.
     Benjamin Hayward, esq.   Worcester.
Rev. Horace Holley,   Boston.
Dr. Isaac Hurd,   Concord.
Mr. Francis Jarvis,   do.
     Phinehas Johnson, esq.   Hampden, Me.
Rev. Samuel Kendall, D. D.   Weston.
Rev. President Kirkland,   Cambridge.
Rev. John Lathrop, D. D.   Boston.
Mr. Phinehas Lawrence,   Lexington.
Rev. Joseph McKean,   Cambridge.
     Tilly Merrick, esq.   Concord.
Deacon James Morrill,   Boston.
     Andrews Norton, A. M.   Cambridge.
Rev. Asa Packard,   Marlborough.
Rev. Hezekiah Packard,   Wiscasset.
Hon. Isaac Parker, esq.   Boston.
Mr. Samuel H. Parker,   do.
     Francis Parkman, A. M.   do.
Rev. John Pierce,   Brookline.
Rev. John Pipon,   Taunton.
Rev. John S. Popkin,   Newbury.
Rev. Eliphalet Porter, D. D.   Roxbury.
Rev. Enoch Pratt,   Barnstable.
     Ebenezer Preble, esq.   Boston.
Rev. John Prince, LL. D.   Salem.
Rev. John Reed, D. D.   Bridgewater.
Rev. Ezra Ripley,   Concord.
Rev. Samuel Ripley,   Waltham.
     Samuel Sewall, A. M.   Cambridge.
Rev. John Simkins,   Brewster.
Rev. Isaac Smith,   Boston.

Mr. Gideon Snow,   Boston.
Rev. Micah Stone,   Brookfield.
     William Sullivan, esq.   Boston.
Rev. Joseph Sumner,   Shrewsbury.
Rev. Seth F. Swift,   Nantucket.
Rev. Thomas Thacher,   Dedham.
Rev. Samuel C. Thacher,   Boston.
Rev. Nathaniel Thayer,   Lancaster.
Rev. Andrew E. Thayer,   Luzern, Pennsyl.
Rev. Joseph Thaxter,   Edgarton.
     Isaiah Thomas, esq.   Worcester.
Mr. John Thoreau,   Concord.
Mrs. Rebecca Thoreau,   do.
Mr. James Thwing,   Boston.
Mrs. Sarah Thwing,   do.
     David Tilden, esq.   do.
Mrs. Sarah Tilden,   do.
Mr. Samuel Torrey,   do.
Rev. Joseph Tuckerman,   Chelsea.
Mr. John Vose,   Concord.
Mr. David Vose,   do.
     Daniel Waldo, jun. esq.   Worcester.
Rev. Henry Ware, D. D.   Cambridge.
* Rev. Samuel West, D. D.   Boston.
     Theophilus Wheeler, esq.   Worcester.
Deacon John White,   Concord.
Rev. Peter Whitney, jun.   Quincy.
Rev. Nicholas B. Whitney,   Hingham.
Rev. Samuel Willard,   Greenfield.
Deacon Jacob Williams,   Burlington, Ver.
Mrs Mary Williams.   Boston.
Rev. Ezra Witter,   Wilbraham.

HONOURARY MEMBERS.

Rev. Dr. Buckminster,   Portsmouth, N. Hamp.
Rev. Dr. Lee,   Lisbon, Connecticut.
Rev. Mr. Leonard,   Canterbury, Connecticut.
Rev. President Saunders,   Middlebury, Vermont.

* Deceased.

SERMON

DELIVERED

AT

THE ORDINATION

OF

THE REV. SAMUEL GILMAN.

A

SERMON,

DELIVERED

AT

THE ORDINATION

OF

THE REV. SAMUEL GILMAN,

TO THE

PASTORAL CARE

OF THE

Second Independent Church in Charleston,

DEC. 1st, 1819.

———

BY JOSEPH TUCKERMAN,

MINISTER OF THE CHURCH IN CHELSEA, (MASS.)

———

CHARLESTON, (S. C.)
A. E. MILLER, PRINTER.
Queen-Street.

SERMON.

WE ARE AMBASSADORS FOR CHRIST, AS THOUGH
GOD DID BESEECH YOU BY US.

2 Cor. v. 20.

AN ambassador is the representative of his sovereign. Christ, as the Ambassador of God, was the representative of God. Commissioned immediately by the Almighty Sovereign,—of whose glory he was a partaker before the world was,—he was peculiarly, God with man. The Apostles, immediately commissioned by our Lord, and invested by him with peculiar powers, were, peculiarly, Christ with men. They were his representatives. They executed his will. And in calling men to repentance, and to the piety and virtue of the gospel, it is their peculiar language, *we pray you, in Christ's stead*. On christian ministers also, who have entered into the labours of the Apostles, devolve the solemn duties of ambassadors for Christ. Our office, therefore, includes all that is most interesting and important, which may be attempted for human improvement and happiness; all that concerns man as an accountable, and immortal being.

Our peculiar relation, both to Christ and to men, is most forcibly expressed in the text. We enter upon the ministry, not indeed as Apostles, peculiarly designated to the office, but from choice of the service; from zealous attachment to his cause; from humble and pure desires to be dispensers of his word, and labourers together with him for the salvation of man. In Christ's stead, we teach the doctrines of his religion; inculcate its duties; and attempt to give impression, and effect, to its promises and threatenings. The number is comparatively small of those, who are disposed to think for themselves upon the subjects, most important as well to their present, as to their future happiness; and the preachers of the gospel, to a considerable extent at least, form the religious sentiments, the motives and morals of those, with whom they are immediately connected. Between ourselves, and the first ambassadors of our Lord, there is indeed the difference,—never to be forgotten,—that under the immediate and supernatural guidance of him by whom they were commissioned, in doctrine and in precept they could not err. But succeeding to their stations and their duties as preachers of his religion, with apostolic simplicity and fidelity we are to impart, according to what we have received. We are separated from the ordinary labours of the world, and by the most solemn acts are consecrated to God and to Christ, for the public services of the church, for the various offices and duties of pastoral care, and for the advancement of all the great purposes of the gospel. The influence, therefore, exerted by ministers of Christ, is necessarily great. Our office, therefore, we likewise consider as greatly important. Happy will be that labourer in the cause of our Divine Master, who feels at once this relation, and these obligations, to him, and to men; and who, in the hour of his final account, will be accepted as an honorable representative of his Saviour and Lord; a faithful messenger of his grace and truth.

To the influence and importance of the christian ministry, let me then direct your attention.

The influence of our ministry, what should it be? What are our just claims upon society?

The time has been,—but blessed be God it has gone by,—when the answer to these inquiries would have comprehended, not only all that private ambition or avarice could demand, but all that the most unrestrained despotism could possess. Happily for us, civil and religious rights are now better understood. At least, in our own favoured country, every man knows that he may elect for himself the place, and the mode of his worship; that he is amenable for his faith to no human tribunal; and that he may follow the guidance of his own conscience, without fear of opposition, while he does not interfere with the conscience, and the rights of others. In addressing you then upon the influence of our ministry, think not that we wish to revive an obsolete doctrine; to assert an antiquated, and long repressed authority. We believe that our Master has given us no claims, which do not grow out of the services we perform, as his servants, for those to whom we minister. We believe that God has entrusted His word to all who have received it; and that, as it is the duty of every one to examine for himself, every one has equally a right, according to the light that God shall give him, to interpret the Scriptures for himself. In preaching His word, therefore, and in the services of our office, the only influence we may ask, or that should be granted to us, is that which all, of unprejudiced and honest minds, will admit should be given to truth ; to our labours in the great cause of christian piety and virtue; to faithful endeavours to enlighten, to reform, and to save those, who are committed to our charge. It is the influence due to our characters, and to our exertions, in our office ; to the christian spirit by which we are actuated, and which we endeavour to extend to those, to whom our ministry may be extended. Beyond these limits, and independent of these means, we desire no authority. But even when thus restricted, is the influence of a faithful minister inconsiderable ? Let me but refer you to some of the most frequently recurring of his services.

And, first, on the morning of the sabbath, cast your eye over the christian world. What a change has the return of this day produced in the thoughts and feelings, the cares and pursuits, the hopes and fears, of at least a great portion of those who believe the gospel? Engaged through the week, many in the exclusive pursuit of business or of pleasure, and all too much inclined, through the deceitfulness of riches, or the lust of other things, to forget God and duty, their constant exposure to death, their responsibility and immortality; all more or less infected with the contagion of the air they have breathed, in the scenes and occupations in which they have sought the happiness of the passing hour; all partaking, though in very different degrees, of the spirit of the world, in whose labours, and calculations, and hopes, and solicitudes, they have immersed themselves; what would be our condition as moral beings, if we were not arrested by this day? if we had not this breathing time in the rapid journey we are pursuing; this hour for self-inspection, for serious remembrance and anticipation? But for the weekly sabbath, how many would soon lose all recollection that they have a spiritual and immortal nature? How many, whom this day recalls to the most solemn exercises, would soon become cold, and earthly, and selfish, and sensual? But important as are its private and domestic services, what would be our sabbaths, without our churches? The public exercises of the house of God bring together the thoughtless, the gay and dissipated, who are ever looking without themselves, and within the narrow limits of the present day, or week, or month, for all which they call enjoyment,—with the sedate, the reflecting, and the pious, who, whether in retirement, or in the bustle of life, are living for eternity; the mere worldling, whose only care is for his immediate gains, with the most devout, whose treasure and heart are in heaven. It is the high object, and the solemn business of a minister of Christ, on this day, to lead the thoughts, the cares, and the devotions of all, to heaven. He stands between his fellow men and their Maker. He has come from the highest exercise of his mind and heart on the great subjects to which he is to excite attention, and from secret communion with God, to direct their prayers; to express their adoration of the Creator and Governor of the Universe; to cherish the sentiment and feeling that we have all *one Father*, are all invited to seek life eternal through *one Saviour*, and that we should likewise have *one Hope*; to offer their united acknowledgements of dependence and gratitude, their penitential confessions, and their supplications for the divine mercy. He dispenses to many those scriptures, which they will not read for themselves; and which from their situations and employments, they could scarcely hear but from his lips. He illustrates and displays, in their power and glory, the doctrines of the gospel; explains and inculcates its precepts; and summons all the contending passions and interests of men to that tribunal, at which we are all at last to be judged. He brings Christ before those who hear him, in all the divine authority with which he was invested by the Father who sent him ; in all the offices of divine love and mercy, in which he is confirming his true disciples, and calling upon all sinners to repent, and to be reconciled to God. He shows them the utter worthlessness of all possessions and honors, compared with an interest in the salvation that is in Jesus; and he exhibits *Christ crucified*,—however to the Jews a stumbling block, and to the Greeks foolishness,—to them that are saved, *the wisdom and the power of God*. By baptism, he initiates the children of believers into the visible church ; and by this act, at the same time, consecrates the parental affections,—the strongest of our nature,—to God their inspirer ; to God our common parent. He distributes the emblems of the body and blood of Christ, in partaking of which we acknowledge ourselves to be one body in Christ; members one of another ; and heirs together of the same inheritance, if we are indeed his disciples. What sources of mutual interest and attachment are these ? What sources of influence to a christian minister? How many owe their strongest impressions of religion to these services; feel their beneficial effects through the week; have their doubts resolved, their fears dispelled, their hopes awakened, and their sorrows consoled! How many have thus been brought from the death of sin, to true repentance; renewed in the spirit of their mind, and made holy to God! How many have thus been advanced in their christian course— their progress towards heaven! In the public exercises of the sabbath, see how many circumstances combine to excite, to exercise and to strengthen the love which binds together a faithful christian minister, and the people of his charge.

Again, a christian minister, if his character is what it should be, in mingling with the people of his care, even when he has not directly in view the performance of official duties, is at once a bond of union by which they are holden together, and by which each is attached more strongly than he would otherwise be, to the objects that demand his highest, his eternal concern. The associations that are thus formed, and of which the heart should never be divested, with the character and objects of a faithful and beloved pastor, are most favorable to christian union, and to the advancement of christian piety and virtue. In his affections; his candour and benevolence; his meek and unostentatious deportment; and his conversation, often on subjects most closely connected with the eternal welfare of man, and always consistent with the principles of religion, they see an image of the master whom he serves; a living illustration of the gospel which he preaches. So should a christian minister deport himself, even in his ordinary intercourse. And can you not conceive of the love that must glow in his heart, when he quits the labours of his retired hours, in which he has been employed in your service,—or rather, in the service of his master for your greatest happiness,—to seek the relaxation of his mind, in affectionate intercourse with the families, to whose best good he has been devoting his thoughts, his reading, his pen, and his prayers? And he anticipates, and receives a correspondent affection.—He anticipates it with peculiar confidence from some. But he receives it also from many, who give scarcely any other indication of their respect for religion. And his is a friendship unmixed with sordid and selfish motives. It flows from the peculiar principles and objects of the relation he sustains to them, as a spiritual pastor and guide; from the close,—may I not say eternal—union of their most important interests. If his character then comports with his office, must not even his most common and familiar intercourse, by attaching the people of his charge to himself, attach them also more strongly to each other? Must it not maintain in life and in action the sentiments and affections, which should peculiarly form and characterize the disciples of Christ? I need not say how precious, to a christian minister, is the

friendship thus contracted. It is inestimable. But is it not obvious, how great
is the influence thus acquired and exerted
by a faithful servant of our Lord?

But not only does a christian minister
exert this indirect, but most salutary influence. In the society that has chosen
him, he is not alone to inculcate principles,
but carefully to watch their operation. He
is in private to perform the duties of a
christian friend, where another would not
perhaps think himself obliged to interfere;
or through fear that the service might be
unkindly received, might shrink from an
office sometimes demanding the best exercise of the judgment, and not always grate-
fully acknowledged, even when performed
with the best intentions. In the ordinary
friendships and connexions of the world,
men generally look to the immediate, or at
best to the temporary advantages and sufferings, that may result from efforts and
sacrifices required of them by duty.—Not
so is it with a faithful minister of Jesus.

He would lead the steps of all into the path of life eternal. Often therefore with secrecy, but with fidelity, he is a monitor of the young; an adviser of the unwary. He is employed in checking vice and encouraging virtue, in their beginnings; and teaching those who are under his care, to associate their first and strongest desires with the prospects and promises of the gospel. And will not they, whom his warnings have saved from many evils, whom his excitements have animated to duty, and enriched with the best satisfactions of man, return the love that is claimed by this well timed friendship? It is also his duty to admonish and to strive with, hardened offenders. And even where he is not successful, great becomes his interest in them; and not unfrequently, strange as it may seem, scarcely less is their respect for, and their attachment to, himself. As a spiritual father among your little children, how many likewise are his means of forming them to the most important knowledge; to piety and virtue;

to present and future happiness? In the children who grow up under his ministerial care, he sees the future members and pillars of the church of Christ. And shall he not,—will he not,—have in return their filial love? But particularly will he feel himself to be bound to those, who have bound themselves to God by the obligations of the gospel. He will spare no labour, he will excuse himself from no service, by which he may strengthen their christian union, and promote their christian progress.—I will only ask, is not the influence thus obtained and exerted as salutary, as it is great and extensive?

Nor are these the only bonds that connect a christian minister with the people of his charge. Let me refer you to scenes and exercises, in which every heart is most susceptible. Let me carry you to the chambers of sickness, and to the house of mourning. It is not the least important of the duties,—let me add, it is not the least valuable of the privileges,—of a faithful christian minister, to be the bearer of the instructions and consolations of the gospel to those, who are suffering under the various trials of life. I would not indeed attach an undue importance to impressions, made upon the heart in the hour of affliction. They are too often the impressions only of fear, and last no longer than the passion that excited them. But they are sometimes permanent, and valuable even as our immortal hopes. Who has not, in seasons of sickness, and mourning, felt his need of a teacher or friend, to whom he could open his heart; express his convictions, his doubts, his anxieties, and his hopes? And how many have sought, or have found without seeking, this friend, in the minister of Christ whom he peculiarly called his own? Yes, if disease visits, or if death enters your dwelling, you expect, and you receive, through your chosen pastor, the supports and consolations of religion. And then, if ever, is the heart peculiarly open to the admission, and the communication of love. Often too, on the bed of sickness, the sleeping conscience awakes; the seared conscience becomes susceptible; the heart that has burned with revenge, is disposed to pardon; the injurer desires forgiveness; the mere worldling feels the worth of the treasures of heaven; and he who has lived most without God, begins to pray, or asks the prayers of those, whose intercessions, he hopes, may be more availing than his own. And how many, in the loss of beloved friends, have felt as they never have before, the importance of immediate preparation for their own departure? In the offices to which a christian minister is called by the afflictions of those who are immediately under his care, how many circumstances are there to excite the highest mutual interest, and to give him influence in their hearts! But when he visits the truly pious, in their days of disease or mourning,—when he sits or prays by the dying bed of those whose departing spirits he may follow with confidence to a better world, how do all the hopes of that world bind together the hearts of those, who thus mingle their sympathies and their devotions? It is impossible that, from these circumstances, great influence should not be derived to a devoted minister of Christ.

Finally, what that is peculiarly interesting and important, is comprehended in, or associated with, any of the most endearing relations of this world, which does not belong also to the relation between a truly christian minister, and the people of his charge? Even their temporal prosperity and adversity, joys and sorrows, are essentially his own; and the facility and comfort with which he is enabled to live, to provide for his family, and to give himself to the objects of his office, are among the chosen and happy objects of their attention and care. But in the performance as well of his daily duties, as of those of the sabbath and the house of God, the infinitely higher concerns of eternity become peculiarly the bonds of their union. A truly christian people will feel, that the health and prosperity of their souls, their preparation for eternity, are the objects of his daily solicitude, his prayers, and his exertions. Thus do their interest in each other, and their mutual love and confidence, partake of the elevation, and strength, and purity of the motives and principles, to which they refer their sacred relation. In their spiritual life, he lives; grows in their spiritual growth, and strengthens in their strength. Their christian improvement is the very life spring of his happiness as a minister of Christ. The influence, therefore, between a faithful christian pastor, and those committed to his care, is mutual. But it is for him, by his fidelity, to make it mutual. In their relation to each other, when sanctified by the principles in which it should be founded, and by which it should be sustained and established, will be felt none of the conflicting passions and interests of the world. They are all *one in Christ*. They love and they follow him, as *a minister of Christ*. And he seeks not *theirs*, but *them*. This is the influence for which we plead. We believe that it is the design of the author and finisher of our faith, that we should possess and cherish it. Nor do we think that, in one well ordered mind, it would even for a moment awaken one feeling of resistance.

Respect for the office of the ministers of religion is universal. It has been felt in all ages, under all forms of religion, and in all countries.—The priests of the early ages of the world were its kings. And under almost all the forms of heathenism, little short of the royal prerogative has been the authority of those, who have regulated the high concerns of the altar. Their supposed favour with the gods has given them a proportionate influence, as intercessors for men. And having thus obtained a direction of the consciences, they have possessed a control of the passions and interests of men, often more entire, than would have been yielded to any merely human wisdom or power. In christendom too, where conscience has been given up to the keeping of those, who, it was thought, could absolve from sin, and open the gates of heaven; and even in protestant christendom, in the sects which have appropriated to themselves all the spirituality of the gospel, all that is most important in truth, and most valuable in the immortal hopes of man; in the sects which indulge a spirit of separation and exclusion, and allow no association of salvation with any other creed or forms than their own; the ministers of religion possess an influence not altogether unlike that of the priests of heathenism. I need not however say that, this is not the proper influence of a christian minister. It is the influence of the spirit of the world, in the disguise of religion. From the early and strong prejudices of education; from the bigotry of some otherwise greatly enlightened, and the ignorance of others; from the natural and unsubdued love of domination in many; and from the very assuming sentiment, that all others must be necessarily and fatally wrong,

because they feel that they are themselves
right, this influence has been, and is extensively given, and exercised; and to it
are every day sacrificed the meekness, the
candour, and the charity of the gospel.
This influence is the mother of persecu-
tion; and where it has been unrestrained
by civil power, it has committed crimes as
enormous as any in the records of human
depravity. May God preserve both you
and us from this dreadful abuse of our
high privileges, as ministers and disciples
of our meek, and lowly, and merciful
saviour!

Where there are national ecclesiastical
establishments, an authority is also possessed by the ministers of religion, which
is in a great measure independent of
ministerial character. I thank God that
we have not such an establishment. Nor
would I for myself, or for my brethren,
have any official influence, but that which
character alone will give us. Respect for,
and attachment to us as ministers of Christ,

ought to cease, as soon as our characters cease to comport with our office. It is altogether a voluntary relation into which we enter with the people of our charge. The minister of a society is chosen by, and not imposed upon the society to which he ministers. This is a circumstance, both to us and those to whom we minister, of inestimable importance. It is a bond of union rarely broken, but by death. Our relation grows out of the mutual affections indulged during a term of probationary intercourse. We know, and then love each other; we love, and are united. And the affection which first connected us, extending with the circumstances that exercise it, and strengthening with time, becomes one of the most powerful bonds of this world. And is the *importance* less great, or less certain, than the influence of a truly christian ministry?

We would not unduly magnify our office. But we are not qualified for this office, if we do not feel the greatness of its interests, and the importance of its duties. Nor could I attempt to illustrate the influence of a faithful minister of Christ, without showing also the importance of his services. But it demands a distinct consideration.

Look upon the world with the eye and heart of a mere man of the world, and you every where see life, activity, the choice of various objects of pursuit, and a thousand various and opposite interests soliciting desire, and animating effort.—But look upon it again with the purged eye of a moral, and an accountable being, and see in this countless multitude how many are awake, only to regard the objects of their senses, and are slumbering over the concerns of their souls. See how many are thoughtlessly rushing on to moral ruin. How many are deluding conscience, and making compromises with God, by hollow professions; and in self-justification for the neglect of piety, plead their morality; or excuse their neglect of morality, by recurring to their offices of piety.—See how many ignorant there are to be instructed; how many poor, whose daily labours leave to them but little command of time, and whose temptations expose them to so much vice and wretchedness, as make them objects for the peculiar solicitude and exertions of a christian pastor. How many, notwithstanding the abundance of their possessions, are anxious only for new accumulations; or are seeking all their happiness in the pride, or the vanity of riches. How many, who will at all hazards be rich, are making shipwreck of faith, of integrity, and of every good affection; and are falling into temptations, and snares, and lusts, which drown men in destruction and perdition.—Look upon the world, even upon that little world in which we live, and the round of which we may daily accomplish,—and ask, what changes does the gospel propose to effect in it? What changes, by the blessing of God, may be effected in it by a faithful ministry? In these, see the interests and duties of our office. *He that converteth a sinner from the errour of his ways, will save a soul from death, and hide a multitude of sins.*

Our ministry derives its importance from the great and most interesting objects of our religion; from the objects for which Christ came into the world, taught, suffered, and died. Do you ask, what are these objects? I answer, to bring sinners to repentance, and the penitent to all the holiness of the christian character. Christianity opens to the eye of our faith a state of ineffable glory, and of eternal improvement. It proposes, even in this world, to infuse into its believers the spirit of heaven. It would give us the spirit of Christ. Christianity is a new spiritual creation. The subjects of the kingdom of Christ are *new creatures.* They are *born again by the word of God.* Christ dwells in their hearts by faith.—Living, they live to the Lord; and dying they die to the Lord. Whether, therefore, they live or die, they are the Lord's. In our exertions to accomplish these objects of our religion, we are *working together with God.* We are *ambassadors for Christ.* We propose, illustrate, defend and apply the doctrines he has taught. We inculcate the duties he has required. We exhort, and we rebuke, only by the considerations, by which our master and Lord enforces obligation, addresses our fears, or awakens and animates our hopes. And what can be so important to every individual of mankind, as these objects of our religion? Yes, these are interests which should be ascendant in every heart; which will make the beggar who obtains them infinitely richer, than all the possessions of the world could make him;—and without which, the most affluent, and the most exalted, will soon find himself to be poor, and miserable, and blind, and naked. It is our business to call the attention of those who hear us to the terms, and the means of their present and their final acceptance. By the mercies, and by the terrours of the Lord, we persuade men. We would make Christ, requiring us to repent,—Christ dying for our sins,—and Christ, our advocate and intercessor in heaven, to be your glory, and your joy. We would make it to be the language and the feeling of every heart, *God forbid that I should glory, save in the cross of our Lord Jesus Christ, by which the world is crucified to me, and I unto the world.*— Will it be denied then, that the design of our ministry is important? It is the great design of God in the salvation, and eternal happiness of men.—Alas! who is sufficient for these things?

Does it seem to any one that these are suggestions of vanity! We acknowledge that it is indeed possible to be vain even of the success, with which we have exposed the emptiness of all the grandeur of the world; with which we have humbled the pride of men; with which we have preached Christ crucified for our sins; or have impressed those who heard us with the awful solemnity of judgment and of eternity. But if this passion be felt, it is because we do not feel the solemnity and importance of our relation to Christ, and to those to whom we minister. It is because we do not feel that we are to account to him for the manner in which we have dispensed his word, and for the intended effects of our ministry. If we cherish the sentiment, —the feeling of this relation, and of the responsibility involved in it, with the deepest humility, as well as the strongest affections and interests of our hearts, we shall *beseech sinners to be reconciled to God.*

If this be not the most affecting view that can be taken of our office, it is certainly one that demands our serious, and very frequent attention. A vain and ostentatious display of ourselves in our ministry; a peculiar regard to our own fame, or influence; and, let me add, a suspicious, an accusing, and a censorious spirit in the ministers of Christ; a disposition manifested to assume the judgment seat, and to condemn; a spirit of enmity and of separation;—is it not the spirit of the world? And will not men of the world, who form their judgments of religion only from what they see of its effects, either infer that they have themselves as much religion as their teachers; or that, in their better morality, they have a deeper and stronger ground of acceptance? Within the circle of his immediate labours, a faithful ambassador for Christ,—a humble, but devoted representative of his Lord,—forgetting himself, and toiling in his master's service; an example of the efficacy of the doctrines he teaches, and of the duties to which he excites others; in the silent, but constant influence of his life and conversation, may make an impression of principles, and exercise a spirit of devotion, in which many, with himself, will rejoice with joy unspeakable in the presence of God. And a minister of Christ,—if to him we may apply the name,—whose passion is vanity or ambition, and whose object is admiration or renown; who preaches of heaven, while his heart is obviously filled with the cares, and his time is principally employed in the business of the world; a minister of Christ, who sacrifices his charity to his zeal, or who exhorts men to deny themselves, and take the cross, while he freely allows in himself the propensities he condemns, and indulges the habits against which he dispenses his admonitions; a minister of Christ, calling upon men to work out *their* salvation, but heedless of *his own;* urging them to a heavenly conversation, while his own breathes only the spirit of the world; a minister of Christ in whom Christ dwells not; what evil may he not occasion? To what guilt may he not be accessary? Who would not shrink from the dreadful anticipation of the account, which such a servant must render to his Master and judge?

Our office is as responsible as it is important. But erroneous sentiments may be, and I think sometimes are, formed of its responsibility. We are to account to God for the temper, and the manner in which we have sought for truth, and in which we have dispensed it. It will be required of us at once, that we have not taught for doctrines the commandments of men; and that we have not failed to declare all that we know, or believe, to be the counsel of God. And God will demand of us, that we have been faithful in the use of all the means and opportunities with which he has entrusted us, of accomplishing the end of our office. But we are not, and cannot be, accountable for effects of our ministry, which are necessarily beyond our control. We are not, and cannot be accountable for the evil of errors, which we have in vain endeavoured to overcome; for vices we have faithfully, but ineffectually resisted. If it be our duty to teach, to admonish, to encourage and to confirm, it is equally the duty of those to whom we minister to hear; to inquire at the word of God, whether these things be so; and accept us in these offices, as far as we are found to be conformed to the instructions of Christ. If we are responsible, not less solemn is the account to be rendered by those to whom we minister. We do not receive souls into our charge, to mould them according to our will. Nor, if we have much self-knowledge, or much of the humility of the gospel, shall we with a dogmatical confidence, feel every peculiarity of our own sentiments, by whatever human names they are sanctioned, to be essential to the salvation of all those who hear us. What we believe to be truth, and important truth, it is indeed our duty to preach, with all the earnestness that should be inspired by all the great considerations that enforce it. But let every one remember and feel, that he also is accountable for these means of grace. Let every one most seriously consider, that he is bound to search the scriptures for himself; to bow his whole soul to their authority; *to work out his own salvation; to give all diligence to make his calling and election sure.* In these views of mutual obligation, and of mutual accountableness, faithful ministers will lose none of their holy ardour, in advancing the cause of their Master; while at the same time they will strongly feel, that it is not for them imperiously to judge and to condemn. And a christian society will feel, that the conscience of their minister is to be left as free as their own; that he can be instrumental of their salvation, only as far as he is an instrument of aiding them in becoming truly christians; and then only can be guilty in their condemnation, when he has not warned sinners of their danger, besought them to repent, and called them to be holy, that they might be forgiven and live.

Is it still thought that we assume too much in giving this importance to our office? Does any one say to us, show us your credentials, before you address us as an ambassador for Christ? Show us the validity of your ordination? We reply that, we have no desire of an imposing name. We claim no authority over any man's conscience. We assert no dominion over your faith or conduct, but that which we can obtain by strength of argument, and the power of persuasion. I have said that, we feel ourselves to be called to this office, by our interest in the christian improvement, and in the eternal salvation of men; by our readiness and desire, forsaking all interests and pursuits inconsistent with it, to live and to die in the service of Christ. And as we attribute all good influence to God, we ascribe this also to His agency. Nor do we pretend that we confer any new powers by the acts of ordination. We do but acknowledge, and, by authority given us by the church in whose name we act, confirm the powers, and rights, and privileges, to the acceptance and exercise of which, he who is to be ordained is invited by those with whom he is to be immediately connected as their minister. In our united prayers we commend him to God; separate him to all the services of the sanctuary; and seek for him the succour and assistance from above, which we feel that he needs. We give to him the right hand of fellowship; welcome him to a share in our labours, our toils, and our joys; and assure him of our sympathy and aid. And in all the departments of the new duties before him, we charge him to be faithful. These rites of our churches are derived from Apostolic usage; and we adopt them, because they are most solemn, most appropriate, and as we believe, most conformed to the order and design of the gospel. If they do not make him whom we thus ordain holy to the Lord, they make him and others, if they have the sensibility of christians, feel that his character and his labours should be holy. With this act of separation, we associate the obligation of all the peculiar duties and services of the christian ministry. In this act, he that is ordained gives up his mind, and heart, and life to the objects, for which the ministry was instituted; the extension and establishment of the dominion of Christ over the faith, and heart, and lives of those, to whom he is to minister. If there is to be a christian ministry, we can conceive of no rites more simple, more impressive, nor more suited to the occasion. They are directly connected in every mind that so conceives of them, with the holiness of our religion, and the corresponding holiness required of all its believers. These are our views of the nature of our office, and of the rites by which we are inducted into it. Nor do we think that they in any measure enfeeble, or weaken the impression of the sentiments, we have expressed of its importance.

By directing attention to the influence, and the importance of our ministry, I have hoped, my dear sir, at once to deepen and confirm the feelings with which you are entering on its duties; and to give a proper direction to the affections and interests of those, towards whom you are particularly to sustain this endearing and solemn relation. You desire, and so you should,—to possess the proper influence of a minister of Christ. You wish to be loved, and to be useful, not from any private and temporal interests, but that you may advance the objects of the gospel. You feel that the importance of the ministry is, the importance of the religious improvement, and the eternal salvation of those, to whom we minister. May you be an able, a beloved, and a successful servant of our great Master and Lord. Without interfering with the charge you are to receive, I may, however, warn you,—and you will kindly receive what is affectionately intended,—neither to desire, nor to exert any influence, for the purity and rectitude of which you cannot appeal to the searcher of hearts. Do not for a moment indulge complacency in the sanctity of character that may be ascribed to you, if you feel that they are deceived by whom you are so estimated. And while you strive with your might, and seek assistance from God, that you may accomplish the purposes of your ministry, let not an undue influence be attached to any of your labours, as if these could be in any degree effectual to the salvation of a single soul, which possesses not the spirit of Christ, and lives not obedient to his laws.

If you be a faithful minister, you will find in your duties a full employment of your time. We may indeed so pass through the round of our office, as to leave much leisure from its services, and yet not expose ourselves to be loudly, or severely blamed. But little to be envied is that ambassador of Christ, however desirable in other respects his condition may be, who has no higher aim, than to avoid the immediate censures of those to whom he ministers. You will watch and labour for the salvation of souls, feeling always that you are to give account of your office. New pleasures await you, and they are the most refined and valuable of this world. But new trials and discouragements are also before you. You are, therefore, to show yourself to be a good soldier, as well as a faithful representative of our Lord. You must be willing to suffer, as well as to toil for our Master. You must feel that the poorest and most obscure, have equal claims upon your care, as the most affluent and respected. You will, therefore, like our Master, preach the gospel to the poor; and by suiting your instructions to their condition and wants, you will yourself become poor, that you may make many rich. While God is the final object of your love, and trust, and devotion, you will strive to make Christ, in his offices and his example, his commands and his promises, dearer to the hearts of them that hear you, than any possessions or relations of the earth. You will live in daily, humble and fervent prayer, that God may guide and strengthen you; that he may assist you in your studies, in your preaching, and in your parochial intercourse; that through His grace, you may have many souls as the reward of your labours; and that you may so preach to others, as not yourself to be cast away. And, *we bow our knees unto the Father of our Lord Jesus Christ, of whom the whole family in heaven and earth is named, that he would grant you, according to the riches of glory, to be strengthened with might by His spirit in the inner man; that Christ may dwell in your heart by faith; and being rooted and grounded in love, that you may be able to comprehend with all saints, the breadth, the length, and depth, and height; and to know the love of Christ that passeth knowledge; and that you may be filled with all the fulness of God!*

BRETHREN OF THIS CHRISTIAN SOCIETY,

We congratulate you on all the auspicious circumstances of this day. May it be a day of increasing gladness in your remembrance! May you and your children have occasion to rejoice in a recurrence to it, in the day of your final account!

It has pleased God, in his inscrutable providence, very early to deprive you of the labours of a young, but greatly beloved teacher and pastor. The affection with which you cherish the remembrance of his intercourse and services, the kindness you have extended to him through the long and distressing term of his illness, the solicitude with which you are constantly seeking information concerning him, and the influence which even at so great a distance, he is still exerting among you are pledges to us that our brother, whom we are now to set over you in the Lord, may also labour among you with a christian hope, of advancing in your hearts and lives the great interests of the Redeemer's Kingdom. We join our fervent prayers with yours, that it will please God mercifully to watch over the revered object of your anxieties and supplications; to soften the pillow of his declining life; to support him in all his trials and sufferings; and when you shall stand with him at that tribunal, at which he must give account of his ministry, and you of your improvement or neglect of it, that he may be accepted as a faithful servant, and you as seals of his ministry, and crowns of his rejoicing.

We are now, by the solemn rites of ordination, to separate this our brother to your service in the Lord. He is the man of your choice. You have given full proof of your affection for him, and of your confidence in him. But let me remind you that, to receive him indeed as a minister of Jesus Christ, you must feel that the importance of his office arises from the importance to your eternal salvation, of that gospel you invite him to preach to you. While his character and exertions shall correspond with the objects of a truly christian ministry, and you shall see him zealously engaged in seeking your religious improvement, and your final happiness, allow him the influence that is due to his care and his labours. He will come into your families, with his heart warm with the affections of the gospel. Receive him then as your pastor, with all the love that should be felt in this endearing relation. But we ask, and we desire for him no other influence, than he can obtain by a heart and life devoted to his duties.— He will be inclined to give a full portion of his time to the social intercourse, in which he hopes to obtain much of the success, and the happiness, of his ministry. But you will not require of him those attentions, which would interfere with the hours that should be consecrated to study. He desires to come to you always as a scribe well instructed unto the kingdom of heaven. Allow him then the uninterrupted retirement demanded for his preparations for the pulpit. If you would gladden his heart, and encourage his hands, you will also attend upon his preaching with constancy, with seriousness, and with earnest desires of self-improvement; with inquisitiveness, but without a disposition to cavil; and respecting his conscience, while you cultivate your own. It will be his duty to preach to you all that he believes is the will of God in Christ Jesus concerning you. It is not less your duty to hear with ingenuous, and with candid minds; with earnest desires of being made wise unto salvation, through faith in Christ Jesus.

If you shall at any time think that he errs, either in doctrine or in conduct, make not his error a subject of public discussion, 'till it has first been thoroughly discussed in private with himself. Innumerable divisions and evils have arisen in families, in the church, and in the world, only from misconception and mistake, which fair explanations at first would have entirely obviated. He comes to you in Christ's stead, to beseech you all to be reconciled to God. Let him, therefore, speak to you with the simplicity and the directness, which mark and characterize the instructions of our Lord and of his apostles. Hear him when he calls upon you to repent; when he admonishes you, *by the meekness and the gentleness of Christ*, that ye *put away all wrath, and anger, and clamor, and evil speaking, with all malice;* and that ye be forbearing and affectionate, not towards one another only, but towards all men; when he warns you, *be not conformed to this world, but be transformed by the renewing of your mind;* when he enforces the command and the promise, *believe on the Lord Jesus Christ, and thou shalt be saved;* when he exhorts you, *put ye on the Lord Jesus Christ;* and *lay hold on eternal life.* Hear him when he invites you to commemorate that love of our Saviour for us, which was stronger than death ; and bring your children to him, that he may initiate them by baptism into the church of our Lord. And let your daily prayers ascend to God for him, that he may be an instrument of bringing you and your children to glory, to honour, and to immortality. Thus, being sanctified and cleansed by the washing of water, and by the word, may you be at last accepted a glorious church, not having spot or wrinkle, or any such thing ; but holy, and without blemish.— Now, therefore, O God, hear the prayer of thy servants, and cause thy face to shine on this thy sanctuary ! Clothe thy priests with salvation, and cause thy saints to shout aloud for joy? And now unto Him that is able to do exceeding abundantly, above all that we can ask or think, according to the power that worketh in us, unto Him be glory in the church by Jesus Christ, throughout all ages, world without end.   Amen!

RIGHT HAND OF FELLOWSHIP

BY THE

Rev. JARED SPARKS,

OF BALTIMORE.

———

THE works and dispensations of God declare his goodness. The smiles of his love beam upon us from every object in nature. The temple of the universe is a magnificent display of his benevolence, no less than of his wisdom and power.

But the love of God is no where more conspicuous, than in the endowments, resources and prospects of his creatures. He has formed us intellectual and rational beings; he has given us powers, which elevate and dignify our natures; he has made us capable of knowing and imitating his perfections. And he has not only bestowed upon us the noble distinctions of reason, intelligence, wisdom, conscience; he has also implanted within us the principles of love, which make so large a part of his own character. These are the principles, which our religion is intended to call forth and improve.

The Saviour of men spake to us in the accents of love. His gospel is an angel of love, which bears on its wings the joyful tidings of peace and good will to men. His religion was intended to influence the heart, to awaken the affections, "to make man mild, and sociable to man," and by causing us to live in peace and concord, to prepare us for a more intimate and happy fellowship in the regions of the blessed. The religion of Jesus Christ has no other object, than the happiness of men. For this, he gave light to a world before in darkness; for this, he suffered and died, and left us a pure, and holy, and perfect example. His life was as spotless as his doctrines were divine. The dews of heavenly instruction distilled from his lips. Compassion for the afflicted, sympathy with the disconsolate, and the desire of doing good to all, prompted every emotion of his soul, and every action he performed. He would have us plant, and nourish the seeds of our own happiness, and enjoy the fruit of our labours. This must be done by a cultivation and exercise of our best affections; by drawing closer the ties of friendship, and multiplying the harmonies of life; by mutual efforts to give activity to the social principle, and to extend the influence of religion.

To promote these objects, the apostles of old were accustomed to give the *right hand of fellowship* to those, who were appointed to be fellow labourers with them in the cause of truth, as a symbol of union and brotherly love. In conformity with this usage of the primitive christians, in the name of the churches, and in compliance with the instructions of the council, which has approved your ordination, I give you this right hand. Take it, my brother, as a token of our love, a pledge of our cordial fellowship, of our warm interest in your welfare, and the success of your ministerial labours. We receive you with gladness to a participation in all the privileges and services, the cares and solicitudes, the satisfactions and hopes of the sacred office, to which you are this day solemnly dedicated. We promise you our consolation and support, as far as our opportunities will allow, and feel assured we shall receive yours in return.

Christians are commanded to preserve a unity of the spirit in the bond of peace. Let this be our aim. It is not a uniformity in opinions, in faith, or in our peculiar notions of metaphysical theology, which is required; but a unity of spirit, temper, feelings and disposition. Whatever may be our speculative opinions, whatever views we may have of the disputed points of doctrine, to whatever religious denomination we may belong, or however widely we may differ in the outward forms of worship; in all that is essential as christians, in all that is essential to purity of heart, holiness of life, and acceptance with God, we may meet as brethren. Here is a bond of union, which may embrace all the followers of Christ. We may all unite in keeping alive the spirit and temper of his religion. We may harmonize in devotion and love to God, in charity and mutual kind offices to one another. We can be of one heart and one mind in a faithful discharge of the duties of piety and of our social relations. May you, and may we all who profess to be the disciples of Christ, endeavour to promote this christian unity, and think it more important, that our lives should be adorned with these essential virtues of our religion, than that we should spend our time in idle differences about words, and forms, and opinions.

In discharging the duties of a minister of Christ, we cannot promise you pleasures without pain, rewards without toil, or anticipations without disappointment. We cannot promise you, that the dreams of hope will always be realized, or that your zeal and exertions will always be crowned with adequate success. But amidst your cares and anxieties, you will be consoled with the consciousness, that you are striving to do all to the glory of God, and for the good of men. While you see the humble, and pure, and gentle spirit of the gospel daily gaining a hold on the hearts of men; while you see charity, peace and concord mingling in their intercourse, and giving a tone to the society around you, do not feel, that your labour is vain.

And now, my friend and brother, permit me to avail myself of the privilege of this occasion, and offer you this hand again, as a testimony of personal friendship and affection. You will not think it a cold or formal offering, nor do I believe it will revive associations, which you would wish to suppress. We have walked together in the groves of science, we have listened to the same voice of instruction, we have searched with mutual labour for the treasures of knowledge, and divine truth. These are the recollections of former times. And even now, it has been the will of Providence, that our lots should be similar. We have left far behind the cherished scenes of our earlier years, the occupations which delighted, and the friends, who consoled and cheered us, to make our residence in a land of strangers. But the cause of truth and of heaven is a universal cause. While we approve ourselves faithful servants of our Lord and Master, and discharge with fidelity the duties of our station, we shall find the stranger our friend, the God of mercy will overshadow us with the wings of his love, sustain us in the hour of trial, scatter the clouds of despondency, and gild with the beams of joy the rising prospects of our future labours.

Christian brethren, and friends of this church and society, allow me to offer you our congratulations on this occasion, and to express the joy we feel in the testimony you have given of your zeal in the cause of christian truth and liberty. Our best wishes are, that you may be built up in the spirit of christian unity and love, and that you may be enlightened with a knowledge of the truth as it is in Christ Jesus. We hope you will always regard it, not only your privilege, but your right and duty, to assert and maintain the freedom wherewith he has made you free. Let his example and instructions, and those of his apostles be your guide. Let your own conviction of the truth, and your own understanding of the word of God, be the measure of your faith ; and whatever others may think and teach, let it be your determination to "read and understand," and "judge of yourselves what is right." Let your value of the truth be known by the candour and earnestness with which you search, and the readiness with which you embrace it. Let your faith be known by your practice; your good intentions by your good actions; your love to God, by your love to men; the sincerity of your religious professions, by the holiness of your lives.

SERMON

PREACHED

AT

THE ORDINATION

OF

THE REV. ORVILLE DEWEY.

A

SERMON,

PREACHED AT THE

ORDINATION

OF

THE REV. ORVILLE DEWEY.

PASTOR OF THE FIRST CONGREGATIONAL CHURCH

IN

NEW-BEDFORD,

DECEMBER 17, 1823.

———

BY JOSEPH TUCKERMAN,

Pastor of the Church of Christ in Chelsea, Mass.

———

NEW-BEDFORD:

PUBLISHED BY ANDREW GERRISH, JR.

BENJAMIN LINDSEY, PRINTER.

....

1824.

TO

THE REV. ORVILLE DEWEY,

AND THE

CHRISTIAN SOCIETY

UNDER HIS PASTORAL CARE,

THIS SERMON,

PRINTED AT THEIR REQUEST,

IS INSCRIBED

WITH SINCERE RESPECT AND AFFECTION,

BY

THE AUTHOR.

NEW-BEDFORD, Dec. 18th, 1823.

SERMON.

HEBREWS I. 1, 2.

God, who at sundry times, and in divers manners, spake in time past to the fathers by the prophets, hath in these last days spoken unto us, by his Son.

In these words, we are taught that Christianity is the last of a series of divine communications to man; and, in the faith that it is a dispensation from God, we have assembled here, to perform one of its most solemn and important rites; the Ordination of a Christian Minister. I avail myself, then, of the occasion, to call your attention, to the *distinctive character, and claims, of the religion of Christ.* In right views of the peculiar character of our religion, we obtain just sentiments of the distinctive character, and objects, of the Christian Ministry. It will shew also, that our religion is worthy of all the efforts and sacrifices, that it may demand, for the maintainance of its institutions; that they are the proper objects of the highest concern of every individual.

The Distinctive Character, and Claims of Christianity : What are they?

First, let us glance at them,—for it is a glance only that we can take of them—*in the manner in which our religion was taught by our Lord.* Happily for us, our Lord's manner of teaching is preserved in the narratives of the Evangelists, which are as original, as distinctive, even as our religion itself.

In this view of our subject, I would remark only, that in the manner in which our religion was taught by our Lord, it was *brought to the severest trial of its truth.* It was shewn also, as it could not otherwise have been shewn, to be *suited to the ever varying exigences of human life; suited to form the heart and character of man to the moral perfection, to which it calls its believers.* We do not, indeed, distinguish it from Judaism, by any of its characters of truth. But, by these we distinguish it from all other religions. And we distinguish it even from Judaism, in its suitableness to the circumstances of all mankind, and to the greatest possible exaltation of our nature.

Let us look, then, at the records of the four Evangelists.

It is worthy of observation, that, to every one who can read them in the language in which they were first written, they are obviously—except one, that of Luke—the writings of men, who certainly were not skilled in composition. Nor is there in one of them an indication of a design to produce, what is called, *effect*. And yet, never was there a narrative, either before, or since the days of the Evangelists, suited to exert any moral power, compared with that which has been, is, and will be exerted, by these simple composures. Their design is single, and uniform. It is, to teach Christianity. And how do they teach it? Not by making a collection of abstract truths. Not by compiling, from the instructions of their Master, what is called, in modern times, a system of christian theology. But, by giving us, what is certainly far better, *a history of Christianity during the life of Jesus;* thus leaving every reader of the New Testament to determine the question for himself, *what is Christianity?* They faithfully relate to us, what Jesus said, and did, and suffered. And not only so. By the perfect artlessness, at once, and the vivacity of their narratives, they make us, as far as it may be done, hearers of his discourses, and witnesses of his miracles and conduct. They exhibit to us Christianity, in its great design, *in the life and character of its author.* And need we, to convince any one of the perfect originality of this character, or of its truth, to extend our appeal beyond the records, in which it is transmitted to us? *

* These remarks may be applied equally to the Acts of the Apostles, and to their Epistles.

The Acts of the apostles are *a history of Christianity*, from the ascension of our Lord, till the seventh year of the emperor

Here is one, who claims to be the *Son of God;* to have *come from God*, that he

Nero; when Paul was taken to Rome, in consequence of his "appeal to the judgment seat of Cæsar." Here are related the transactions of the Apostles in solemn council; the effusion of the Holy Spirit upon them, according to the promise of our Lord; their preaching and miracles; the resistance which the Jews continued to oppose to our religion, and the conversion of many ten thousands of them; the very peculiar circumstances under which Peter was constrained to preach the gospel to the Gentiles; the conversion and apostleship of Paul; his travels, and preaching; the persecutions he endured; his trials before the civil authorities; and his voyage from Cesarea to Puteoli, on the bay of Naples, from which place he went by land to the imperial city. This is, in truth, a most precious book. Here, as in the narratives of the Evangelists, our religion is given to us, *in association with facts and reasonings;* and we see it, in almost every sentence, accumulating new evidence of its truth, and its power; and in the preaching of the Apostles, breathing the very spirit of Jesus. It is in this all pervading, life giving, heavenly spirit of their instructions, that we see what Christianity was in the days of its apostles. Here our religion is taught, as nearly as it could be in the circumstances in which the apostles were, as it had been taught by our Lord. Here—and the remark applies equally to the epistles—it is carried through all the scenes of difficulty and suffering, through which its preachers passed; and its doctrines and duties are to be studied in connexion with the circumstances, with which they stand recorded. There is an expansion thus given to our views of all the subjects on which the apostles taught, which we could not have obtained from any other mode of presenting them to us. To our view of the internal evidence of our religion, derived from this mode of its transmission to us, Paley has done ample justice in his Horæ Paulinæ. It is an argument, which infidelity has not attempted might bring the last dispensation of his will to mankind.   He professes, that *he is*

to answer; and it is scarcely less satisfactory, than a mathematical demonstration.   But let any one pass from the four gospels, to this book, and read it throughout with singleness of eye and of heart; and in the characters, preaching, and conduct of the apostles, he will see Christianity to be—with many new illustrations indeed, but still—precisely what it was in the teaching of our Lord.   He will see it to be, not a mere form of doctrine, or a code of laws; but, *a scheme of divine operation for the renewal and sanctification of the heart and character of man; for the salvation of a world of sinners.*   He will here see our religion at war, not only with idolatry, and with spiritual wickedness in high places; but with ignorance in all its degrees, and with depravity in all its forms.   He will find it, not in metaphysical disquisitions, but *in the actual agency of Christ in the concerns of his church; in the increasing clearness and force with which the great designs of Christ are developed, as they respect each individual, and all mankind; as they respect this world, and the life to come.*   This mode of communicating to us our religion, seems to me to be, of all that can be supposed, the most suited to display the wisdom, and power, and mercy of God; the most suited to form the character, to which it addresses its promises.

The grand arsenal of theological controversy, is in the epistolary department of the New Testament; in which were *some things hard to be understood,* even in the days of the apostles. How much harder still then is it, at this time, to arrive at that certainty in regard to these obscurities, which will justify any one in pronouncing authoritatively upon their import? One thing, however, I think we may affirm without fear; which is, that these epistles contain no *doctrine,* which is not contained in the teaching of our Lord, as it is transmitted to us by the Evangelists.   The author and finisher of our faith did not leave *in the Father*, and that *the Father is in him;* that *the Father has sanctified, and*

a defective religion, and commission his apostles to perfect it. In regard both to doctrine, and to duty, there is, and must be, throughout the New Testament, a perfect unity of character. Any contrariety that may appear in these epistles, is the result of the peculiar circumstances under which the apostles taught; the peculiar objections to our religion which they had to obviate; the misconstructions of christian truth, which they had to correct; the inquiries of churches—now, perhaps, but very imperfectly understood by us—which they had to answer; and the contentions, which they had to settle. Forget that these epistles are "accommodated to the disputes and controversies, the errours and false notions, which prevailed when they were written," and we shall be exposed to as many misconceptions of their true import, as they were themselves designed to expose, and to remove.

"The general method observable in these apostolic letters is, *first*, to discuss the particular point debated in the church, or among the persons to whom they are addressed, and which was the occasion of their being written; and in *the next place*, to give such exhortations to every christian duty and virtue, as would be at all times, and in every church, of necessary and absolute importance; paying a particular regard to those virtues, which the disputes that occasioned the epistle might tempt them to neglect. Now the former part of these epistolary writings cannot be rightly understood, but by attending carefully to the state of the question there determined. Therefore the errours and vain disputes concerning Faith and Works, Justification and Sanctification, Election, Reprobation, &c., which have so long vexed, and distracted the minds of christians, have all arisen from one grand mistake; that of applying to themselves, or to other particular persons *now*, certain *sent him into the world*, for the instruction and salvation of men; that he came *to seek and to save that which was lost;* that he *speaks the words*, and *does the work of his Father;* that *he can do nothing of himself;* but that God has given him power to bring to eternal life, and to eternal happiness, all who receive, and obey him.* See, then, how the Evangelists carry our religion through all the trials, through which our Lord himself was carried.

In the four gospels, we have narratives of the conversation and conduct, as well of the enemies, as of the friends of Jesus. Here, in almost every direction, we see new adversaries of his person, and of his

phrases or passages, which plainly referred to the *then* state and condition, not of particular persons, but of whole churches, whether Jewish or Gentile, of those times. Perplexed and puzzled with these knotty points, many well meaning christians have been drawn from paying a due regard to those moral, and weighty exhortations, which are most easy to be understood, and of infinite obligation to be put in practice." PYLE. *See Percy's Key to the New Testament, p. 80.*

* John xiv. 10, 11, and x. 36, 37.—Luke xix. 10.—John iii. 35, and v. 19–30.

cause; new combinations forming against him; new artifices adopted to ensnare him in his words, to disappoint him in his purposes, to destroy his influence, and to justify designs upon his life. Here we are told of the occupations and weaknesses, the doubts and credulity, the disputes and contentions of his apostles; of the treachery of one of them; of the presumption of another, his cowardice, and denial of his Master; and of the faithlessness of all of them, when they forsook him and fled. And here are related the grounds of the opposition of those who rejected him; their machinations; and their final success in his crucifixion. Greater embarrassments, and more formidable obstacles, than were those which our Lord had daily to meet and to overcome, are not even to be imagined. And yet he established his religion. How?

The two methods adopted by him for this end were, *preaching*, and *conversation*. He is night and day surrounded by multitudes, but he never courts observation, and never shuns it. He teaches in the temple, in the synagogue, in the house, in the streets, and in the fields; varying his instructions, and manner of imparting them, with all the varying circumstances of every occasion.—Now, he is dispelling ignorance by the most familiar and condescending explanations; and now, combatting prejudice and errour, with the most powerful reasonings. Now, he is indirectly communicating by parables, what they who heard him, would indignantly have repelled, if it had been more directly taught; and now, he is explicitly announcing the most glorious, and the most solemn truths, as those around him were prepared to receive them. Now, he is encouraging the timid, strengthening the feeble, and animating those who have begun well; and now he is pouring the wine and oil of his consolations into the wounded heart. Now, in language as sweet as can be conceived to be that of heaven, he is dispensing promises, which comprehend all that can be hoped for in heaven; and now, in accents only less terrible than will be those, with which he will at last say to the impenitent, *depart ye cursed!* he pronounces the most dreadful condemnation upon the obdurate enemies of truth and virtue. Here is a zeal, a tenderness, and a compassion, of which there had been no example. No compromise is made with a single sin. No sinner, whatever may be his rank, or his pretensions, is spared. Nay, it is against the very religionists of the age, the proud asserters of their own piety, that he directs his most solemn woes. The design of Jesus is, to establish the *kingdom*—the perfect moral government—*of God*, in every heart. Against secret, and open opposition, therefore, he exposes all that is evil, not alone in the prevailing character of the time, and in established usage, but in fluctuating opinions; in affections and desires; and in all the inducements, and motives, of those who heard him. He lays bare all that hypocrisy attempts to cover; and exhibits sin as a disease of the soul, threatening spiritual death. He declares himself to be the Great Physician, who alone can administer a remedy, that will save from moral death; the death of happiness. Here see the doctrines and duties of our religion, taught in connexion with circumstances, which give to them the greatest possible illustration and power. Can a manner be conceived of proposing religious instruction to man, in which it will be brought to a severer trial; in which duty, in the ever changing circumstances of human temptation, could have been more powerfully enforced; or excitement and comfort, in all our afflictions, more effectually administered?

It is a very remarkable peculiarity of our Lord's teaching, that he seldom asserts his divine mission, or declares himself to be the Messiah, but when peculiar circumstances compel him to it. He prefers to leave the question of his claims to be *felt*, in his *instructions*, and in his *works*. And what were his works? He is every day performing the most stupendous *miracles*.

They are performed, too, as well before his most inveterate enemies, whose investigation of them he challenges, as before his chosen followers. They are performed with the same simplicity, with which God said, *let there be light !* and there was light. And they have the same character of benevolence and mercy, which distinguishes all his instructions. They inspire as well the warmest love to himself, and the most active compassion towards every sufferer, as conviction of his own divine authority. Now I ask, if it be not also very remarkable, that, neither in their accounts of the teaching, and miracles of our Lord, nor in anything that they have said of his actions, or sufferings, the Evangelists have expressed one emotion of admiration of his character; nor have employed an epithet, for the excitement of admiration of it in others. Like himself, they have left his character and authority to be *inferred*, and *felt*, from what is *seen*, and *heard*. Little to be envied is that mind, which is insensible to this peculiarity of our Lord's conduct; and of those records, in which a knowledge of it is conveyed to us.

I will adduce but one other peculiarity of the manner in which our Lord taught his religion. It is, however, a circumstance, to which too much importance cannot be attached; which has no parallel in any other religion; and, in the disregard of which, it is impossible to form a just conception of Christianity. The circumstance to which I refer is, that *our religion was taught, and is to be sought, in the example and life of Christ*.

It will be conceded, that the precepts of Jesus comprehend all the moral duties of man; all that man owes to his Maker, and to his fellow-creatures; and that these precepts, received as the will of God, and faithfully applied to every part of disposition and conduct, would form *a perfect man*. It will be conceded too, even by one who doubts of the divine mission of our Lord, that these precepts, considered apart from our Lord's character and life, and viewed alone in their bearings upon the occasions on which they were given, and the individuals to whom they were applied, are obviously *adapted* to do more for the subjection of all evil passions; more to purify the heart in all its sources of feeling and of action; more to raise man to a moral resemblance of God; to bring universal peace upon earth, and to inspire a hope full of immortality,—a happiness which we could all wish should be immortal,—than had ever before been done, or attempted; or, than had ever entered the thought of man. The most enlightened reason, acting upon human experience, from the time of Jesus till this hour, has not discovered a religious, or moral obligation, which is not plainly comprised in his instructions. Take the fact, then, as unquestionable, and certainly, not less extraordinary, that there is not a duty that he required, repentance alone excepted, which he did not practice. Do we then see in our Lord *absolute moral perfection?* How shall we account for this phenomenon? It is a perfection, too, that is attained, as it must be in ourselves, in the highest degree in which we may arrive at it in this world, by *difficulty*, and *suffering*. We see him, at almost every step of his way, meeting with new impediments, and with many, that are apparently insurmountable; but always rising in moral greatness, and in moral loveliness and attraction, in proportion to the resistance of the circumstances under which he is acting. Is not ours, then, a religion peculiarly suited to the exigences of a state of weakness, temptation and suffering? Could one uncommissioned, and unaided by God, have so taught, and so lived, as did Jesus?

I would ask any ingenuous man, who has never carefully read the gospels, and who is sceptical upon the question of the divine authority of our Lord, to make the attempt to read them with an unbiassed mind; and then to say, whether in the nature of things, it be possible, that Christianity could have been a fabrication of the Evangelists; or whether, on the sup-

position that our Lord taught in Judea,—
the only conceivable one upon which we
can account for these narratives,—it be
possible, with any part of his conduct to
reconcile the idea of imposture; or to
impeach one of his instructions, as unworthy of a communication from God?
Here is no mysterious oracle, uttering
dark responses, capable of various con-
struction, and accommodated to all the
uncertainty of future events. Here is no
assumption of authority, independent of
evidence as unequivocal, as miraculous
power, and perfect holiness and virtue,
can make it. Christianity lives, and acts,
and inspires life, in the examples and facts
with which it is associated. And has any
other religion, in the character and life of
its author, a support of its claims, for a
moment to be compared with that of the
religion of Christ? How, then, I ask
again, shall we account for this character,
and for this religion? How, but by the
admission that he was, what he assumed
to be, *the Son of God.*

In the *second place*, I would remark, that it is a distinctive circumstance in the character of Christianity, from which also it derives distinctive claims, that *in all its doctrines, it addresses itself directly to the reason, and judgment, of all mankind.*

In all the dispensations of God to man, that are recorded in the Old Testament, he has appealed to these highest principles of human nature. But Judaism, as far as it is distinguished from Christianity, was intended to be a local, and temporary dispensation. In these parts of it, therefore, it could not have approved itself to the judgment of *all men*, had the attempt been made, to obtain for it an acknowledgment of its universal obligation. Its great design was, to preserve in the world the knowledge, and worship of the one true God; to teach the purest principles and rules of virtue, which the Jews, as God's people, were then capable of receiving; and to be preparatory to the more spiritual dispensation, in which it was God's purpose to reveal himself to *all mankind.*

All beside, in Judaism, was but incidental to this design, and passed away at the introduction of Christianity. But in its addresses to the reason and conscience of man, our religion looks far beyond Judaism, and it overlooks every other religion. It has in it nothing that is local, nothing that is partial. It does not indeed profess to be, exclusively, a new religion ; but rather, *the completion of the plans of God, for the moral renovation of the world.* It assumes, therefore, from the revelations that preceded it, all that was intended to be perpetual ; and proposes, with what itself reveals, to aim at universal empire. How ? By requiring implicit faith ? No. But by calling upon all men to *understand* its doctrines, as well as to believe them. By teaching doctrines, which, the more they are examined, are found more to illustrate the infinite wisdom, the perfect impartiality and justice, and the adorable love and mercy, of God. Its evidence, arising from the reasonableness of its doctrines, is as broad as are its claims; as deep as are its eternal interests.

That religion itself belongs to human nature,—that it makes a part of what is properly to be denominated human nature, —is demonstrated by the fact, that in no age, or country, of which we have any records, or information, has man been found without religion. Even where his intellectual powers have obtained only that partial development, which enables him to secure for himself few advantages, or comforts, above those of the animals with which he shares the forests, undisturbed but by his contests with them; and where his moral capacities, or rather, his moral exercises, give him no very honourable claims of superiority over the creatures, whose attachment to each other, whose gratitude, and whose fidelity, we do not ascribe to moral principles; even in the most ignorant, and most degraded state of human society, we find *religion*. Man everywhere has, and at all times has had, a feeling of his dependence on a power, or powers,

superior to his own. He has sought to
obtain the favour, and to avert the displeasure, of these great agents, to which
he has felt himself to be in subjection.
Let the opponent of revelation say, if he
please, that in every form in which religion
exists among men, it is fairly to be ascribed, not to the deductions of reason,
but to the uncontrollable operation of *fear;*
and that, deprive man of his fears, and
you equally deprive him of religion. Still,
it is not to be denied, that the principle,
whatever it may be, to which the influence
of religion is to attributed, is, and ever has
been, *universal.* It is as essential a principle of human nature, as is desire, or love.
And, so far has been reason, in the progress of society, from discovering that the
fears, or the principles of our nature, call
them what you will, in which religious
feelings have their origin, are groundless,
and unworthy of an improved condition of
our race, that where men have been unenlightened by revelation, the number both
of gods, and of rites for their worship, has

been increased, with the arts and refinements of civilization. Yes, the very efforts of reason, for the discovery of the mind, and designs of God; even the gods that have been worshipped; the temples that have been reared to them; the altars that have been raised; the smoke of every sacrifice, and the prayers of every offerer of it; all these bear witness, with the unmixed fears of the most ignorant superstition, that the necessity of religion is founded deeply in our nature; that religion belongs to human nature. Even the desire of a revelation has been felt, and expressed, where its excitement can be ascribed only to the actings of reason, upon the indications of a moral government; and the probabilities which nature suggests, of a life beyond the grave.* Is it not reasonable to suppose, then, either if

* We are told of the most distinguished moral philosopher of heathen antiquity, that, having met one of his young disciples going into a temple to pray, and seeing him to be very pensive, and with his eyes fixed on the ground, he asked him, of what he was thinking? The inquiry led to a discussion on the subject of prayer. I quote a few sentences which we find in the close of their conversation.

man cannot, without supernatural aid, attain
the religious knowledge that he wants, and

Socrates. Do you not remember that you told me you were
in great perplexity, through the fear that you should at unawares
pray for evil things, while you designed to ask only for good?

Alcibiades. I remember it very well, Socrates.

Socrates. You see that it is not at all safe for you to go into
the temple to pray, in the condition in which you now are, lest
God, hearing your blasphemies, should reject yonr sacrifices;
and to punish you, should give you what you would not have.
In my opinion, therefore, it is much better that you should be
silent; for I know you well. Your pride,—for that is the soft-
est name that I can give to your imprudence,—your pride, I say,
probably will not permit you to use the prayer of the Lacede-
monians,—who desire the gods *to give them that which is comely,
with that which is good.* Therefore it is altogether necessary
that you should *wait for some one to teach you how you ought
to behave yourself,* both towards the gods, and men.

Alcibiades. And *when will that time come,* Socrates? And
*who is he that will instruct me? With what pleasure shall I
look upon him!*

Socrates. He will do it, who takes a true care of you. We
read in Homer, that Minerva dissipated the mist that covered
the eyes of Diomede, and prevented him from distinguishing
God from man. So it is necessary, in the first place, that he
should scatter the darkness that covers your soul; and after-
wards give you the remedies that are required, to enable you to
distinguish between good and evil.

Alcibiades. Let him scatter this darkness of mine, and do
whatever he pleases. I abandon myself to his conduct, and am
ready to obey all his commands, provided I may but be made
better by them.

  Dacier's Abridgement of Plato. *Second Alcibiades.*

40

needs; or having once possessed, has lost it; that God *would* reveal himself to his intelligent, and moral offspring? Admit that it is, and we fear not any investigation that can be made, of the reasonableness of the doctrines of our religion.—*Hear, and understand*, is the language of Jesus to all to whom he addresses his doctrines. *Prove all things*, says the great apostle of the Gentiles; and *hold fast that which is good.*

Without entering minutely into a consideration of christian doctrines,—which the time forbids,—let me ask you, *first*, to *compare the actual character and condition of man in this world, with the views which are presented of them in our religion.*

The principle, which runs through all the preceding dispensations of God, is also fundamental in Christianity, that *the whole world lieth in wickedness;* that, *all have sinned, and come short of the glory of God;* and, *if we say that we have no sin, we deceive ourselves, and the truth is not in us.* This principle, everywhere recognized in our Lord's teaching, must everywhere be kept in view, when we are considering his instructions. In the eye of Jesus, man is a being of exalted moral powers, and moral relations. He is a child of God; and designed for an immortal existence of moral exercises, and of moral happiness. But he is a being too, equally wonderful in his weaknesses; in his ignorance; in the strength and perversion of his passions; in his subjection to sense, and to appetite; in his proneness to the earth, and to the lusts and vices of the world. In the view of Jesus, sin is a disease, which has extended to the whole of our race. He says nothing, indeed, of the origin of moral evil. It is a question which has nothing to do with practical religion. His great concern is with the fact, *man is, everywhere, a sinner.* He is therefore, everywhere, to be *reclaimed*, and *renewed.* In forming our judgment, then, of christian doctrine, as far as it respects the character and condition of man in this world,—and this is a greatly important view of it,—let history, let observation, let experience give their testimony. The appeal is to facts, and it is addressed to every heart. We ask only, that every individual, in determining the question, are you, or are you not, *a sinner*, should also fairly consider, what are the moral powers which God has given him; and what are the duties, which, in consistency with these powers, God may at last most justly demand of him.

Again, let us view our religion in *its great designs in regard to mankind.*

What are they? Nothing less than the recovery of man from sin; the renewal of every heart from all that is evil; the subjection of every passion to the will of God; the control of every thought; the sanctification of every affection. It would transfuse into every one who receives it, the very spirit of Christ. It would exalt each one, as nearly as he can be brought, to *the measure of the stature of the fulness of Christ.* It is the design of our religion, not merely to establish a more perfect system of ethics, than had before been taught, and to bring immortal life to the light of perfect day ; but, by its instructions concerning the character and government of God, its warnings and threatenings against sin ; and its descriptions, as peculiar, of the character and happiness of heaven ; to bring man to the highest moral exercises ; to the most perfect virtue ; to the purest devotion ; and to *preparation* for heaven. It teaches that, *without holiness, no flesh shall see the Lord;* and, it would make every man, *a partaker of the divine nature.* What, then, has reason to adduce against these designs? It is said, they are impracticable? Infidelity cannot bring another objection against them, that is even plausible. They are not only consistent with the worthiest sentiments that we can form of God, but they give to these sentiments the strongest exercise, in every heart that feels them. They are not only consistent with the highest capacity of our nature, that of indefinite religious and moral improvement ; but they prescribe the only rule, by which the greatest possible progress can be secured ; by which the relative perfection, of which we are not without examples, may be attained in this world.

It is a poor and low conception of our religion, that its end, in regard to us, is accomplished, either by any external observances; or by a piety and virtue which we may approve, when measured by any other standard than that of the gospel. The great peculiarities of Christianity are to be seen, in its adaptation to the circumstances of *a world of sinners;* and in its provisions for the forgiveness, and acceptance of God, which it would obtain for us. It proposes to produce as great a change of heart and character in every individual, as would be effected, if he were all that the instructions of Christ could make him. Cast out of Christianity what is remedial in it—what concerns its purposes and means of mercy for sinners, and it is a religion for angels; for intelligences, pure as those of the heaven to which it calls us. Is reason, then, offended, that great means should be employed, for ends so great as are proposed by our religion?

Is reason offended, that God should send *his Son*, for the restoration, and salvation of men?

Christianity teaches, also, that *God will give his holy spirit to them that ask him.* And is it unreasonable, that creatures who are exposed to so many temptations, and who are called to such attainments; that children of such a Father, in their desires and endeavours to obtain his favour, should be permitted to ask, and should be assured of receiving, the assistance which they need from him? If we are called to the holiness of the first disciples of our Lord; to the same willingness to forsake all, if it be necessary, in order to follow Christ; and if we have to struggle with the same opposing interests of passions, with which they had to contend; do we, less than they did, require the supports, and excitements, and consolations of the spirit of God?

Or, I would ask, has reason anything to bring against the doctrine, of *the death of our Lord Jesus Christ for us;* the doctrine, that *his blood was shed for the remission of sins.* It is indeed most irrational to suppose, that the innocent, the holy Jesus, died as *a substitute* for sinners; that he suffered the *punishment* of their sins. *Punishment* necessarily implies *guilt*, in him who is the subject of it; nor will the term admit of application to the sufferings of one who is innocent, whatever he may endure in the cause of the guilty. Nor is there a word like this, in the teaching either of our Lord, or of his apostles, on this deeply interesting, and important subject. Neither is there a word in the New Testament, of the imputation of our sins to our Lord, or of the imputation of his righteousness to those who believe in him. *He that doeth righteousness,* and he only, *is,* or can be, *righteous.* But it is most true, and worthy of all acceptation, that our Lord died *to redeem,* or to deliver *us from all iniquity; and to purify us unto himself, a peculiar people,* ZEALOUS OF GOOD WORKS. He died for us, because *he loved us;* and to manifest the love and mercy of his Father, who *sent him to bless us, by turning us away, every one, from our in-iquities.* The death of our Lord, therefore, is designed to be a means of our forgiveness, by bringing us to true *repentance ;* and thus, *cleansing our conscience from dead works, to serve the living God ;* by exercising in our hearts a corresponding love of God, and of our Saviour ; and by exciting us to all the duty, to which he calls us. In this view of it, the death of our Lord operates for our redemption, or the forgiveness of our sins, by its influence in delivering us from the power of sin ; and by forming us to the character, to which he promises forgiveness, and the happiness of heaven. And this influence it will exert upon us, in proportion as we feel our entire dependence on God's mercy, for acceptance in the day of our account, and for final blessedness. We fear not, then, to bring these, and all the doctrines of our religion,—let them but be derived pure from the scriptures in which they have come down to us,—to the test of unperverted reason. Let passion, let

41

prejudice be repressed, and all the doctrines of Christ will have all the evidence to our minds, which consistency with unquestionable facts, with all that is known of God, and with all that is known of our own nature, can give to them.

Much errour has resulted from the idea, that it was a design of revelation to teach the metaphysical nature, and essence of God. Hence, there has been as bold a spirit of enterprise, and of adventure, in the work of making discoveries in revelation, as in any of the departments of natural science; and poor, short sighted creatures, who know not in what consists the vitality of a plant, have attempted to fathom the depths of the infinite, and eternal Mind. Alike fruitful too of errour is the supposition, assumed as it has been, as an elementary principle in reasoning upon the subject, that it was a design of the death of our Lord Jesus Christ, to *induce God*, unwilling in himself, to the exercise of compassion, and to the bestowment of forgiveness. But so taught not

our Lord. All that had been revealed of
the divine character, will and purposes, he
takes for granted ; and reasons from it, as
known and established truth. The simple
unity of God ; his almighty power, and
perfect wisdom and goodness ; his moral
government of the world ; his design to
bless, and to reward the good, and to
punish the obdurately wicked ; and, his
placability,—his willingness to pardon the
penitent ;—these great doctrines, instead
of being columns in the christian church,
are, in fact, materials of its foundation.
*Thus saith the Lord, the king of Israel, and
his Redeemer, the Lord of hosts ; I am the
first, and I am the last ; and beside me there
is no God. I am he that blotteth out thy
transgressions for mine own sake, and will
not remember thy sins.** Is it asked, then,
what are the peculiar doctrines of Christianity? I answer, they are the doctrines,
that the knowledge and worship of the one
true God, which had been confined to

* Isaiah xliv. 6, and xliii. 20.

Judea, is to be made *universal;* that *Jehovah* is equally the *God of the Gentiles,* as *of the Jews;* and that he is to be worshipped, not by oblations and sacrifices, but *in spirit*, and *in truth.* And is it little that we owe to Christianity, in its design to spread the knowledge and worship of the one true God, *over the world?* They are the doctrines, that *if we confess our sins, God is faithful and just to forgive us our sins, and to cleanse us from all unrighteousness;* * and that, *whosoever believeth on the Son of God, and followeth him, hath everlasting life.*† The peculiar doctrines of Christianity are to be sought, not in new definitions of God, for our Saviour has not given them; nor in a division of the divine nature into distinct persons, for there is no such division in any of his instructions concerning the Father; nor, in the notion, that God was, in himself, implacable, for it is not authorized by an expression of the Old, or of the New

---

* 1 John i. 9.　　　† John iii. 15, 18, 36; and viii. 12.

Testament. No. They are to be sought in the abundant language of our Lord, and of his apostles, concerning the underived love of our Father in heaven, towards his guilty family of man ; that love, which was manifested, and proved, peculiarly by the mission and instructions, the sufferings and death of Christ, in the cause of our salvation. They are to be sought, in the instructions of our Lord and his apostles, concerning that *repentance*, to which all are called, to whom a knowledge of his religion is extended. They are to be sought, in all that we are taught in the New Testament, concerning the christian character; concerning the character of heaven ; concerning the certainty, and the principles, of the judgment that awaits us, and all mankind ; the future, and tremendous consequences of unrepented sin ; and the unspeakable, the eternal felicity, promised to the penitent,—to the obedient. Here, then, are appeals, not to speculative philosophers, to whom religion is a mere theory of faith, but, to men who would reason of the concerns of their eternal well-being. Here are instructions, suited to the most exalted conceptions that can be formed of God; suited to our nature, and condition; suited to secure the immortal happiness of all, who shall be brought under their influence. And is not this, we may boldly ask, a religion, which has, in itself, a complete justification of all the claims it can make upon us?

From very early time, it has been the folly, the guilt, and the misery of man, that he has thought that he could improve the revelations of God, by bringing them into another form, than that in which it pleased the Divine Being to give them; by making clear what God has left obscure; by obtaining, through a process of inference, what it has not pleased God to teach; and by establishing, what is called order, and harmony, in his dispensations. By this most daring presumption, our religion suffered greatly, even in the days of the apostles. There were, even then, those who thought that Christianity was very imperfect, and defective, without the rites of Judaism; and others, that it required the prevailing principles of the philosophy of the time, to make it altogether worthy of God. Nor were there wanting those, who thought that the very rites of heathenism might be advantageously appended to it, in view of its great object, of bringing *all* to the acknowledgment of its truth, and the observance of its worship. And, when the New Testament, at the reformation, had been rescued from its incarceration in the cells of monks, and published in languages in which the people of Christendom might read it, and judge for themselves concerning religious truth, and right, and duty; it was immediately, and strongly felt, that if the religion of Christ were to be learned by the people from the New Testament alone, they would have no just conception of its design, and no order, and consistency, in their faith. It was felt, and feared, that these records of the life and teaching of our Lord and his apostles, might lead to errours in opinion, which it was as desirable to prevent, as it had been to escape from those, from which the reformers themselves had but just been emancipated. It was therefore . one of the first objects of the great agents in the work of the reformation, to bring the doctrines of these immethodical records into *a system;* and from that time to the present, system has followed system, and creed has been succeeded by creed, till almost every variety, and contradiction of opinion, has obtained, in one and another of christian sects, the dignity of a christian doctrine; and has its advocates, who claim for it the sanction of the authority of Christ. Nay, such has been the ascendancy, which these systems of human device have obtained; so extensively, in regard to them, has the New Testament been read, and studied; so much has it been the object of preaching to teach, and to maintain them; and so exclusively, with a view to them, have a large part of the churches of the christian world been erected, and supported; that few, comparatively, if asked, what are the great characteristic doctrines of Christianity, would think of referring immediately to the New Testament for an answer. The resort would rather be, to the peculiarities of the sect to which they belong. But, blessed be God! a happier era has begun, and is advancing. Not only is the right of every individual acknowledged, to inquire for himself, what is christian doctrine; but the duty is also extensively felt, and its corresponding obligations. The horizon of Christendom is brightening everywhere around us; and our conviction is receiving all the strength, which fact, as well as promise, can give to it, that the grain of mustard seed that was sown by the Son of God, will become a tree, which will cover the hills with its shadow; which will send forth its boughs unto the sea, and its branches to the ends of the earth.

The *last circumstance* of Christianity which I will mention, from which it derives its distinctive character, and which justifies all the claims it can possibly make upon us, is, that *it meets, accounts for, and proposes to accomplish, all the wants of our immortal nature.*

The wants of our immortal nature. Does any one ask, what are they? I answer, they are the wants which this world never satisfied, and never can satisfy. There are indeed wants of our nature, which the objects of this world, and the economy of God's daily providence, were designed to accomplish. But these are the wants which we have in common with the creatures below us. Deprive man of his rational, and moral nature, and you prepare him, in these objects, and in this economy, to find satisfaction. It is found, by the creatures that are without reason, and without a moral nature. But improve reason, and advance society in knowledge, and in arts, and proportionally, you multiply *wants;* you increase the impatience, the restlessness, and the dissatisfactions of want. See how many, how craving, how importunate are the demands, even of the most prosperous, whose hearts, and whose hopes, rise not above this world! How many, too, are the reverses, and the afflictions, in which the heart implores consolation and support, that the world cannot give! See, also, the wants of our immortal nature, as they are shewn by the excited conscience of an awakened sinner! See them, as they crowd upon one another, and contend for utterance, when the feeling is brought home with power, of the certainty, and the nearness, of death! Other religions, to the extent to which they recognise these wants, of course propose to meet, and to supply them. But it is Christianity, and Christianity alone, that penetrates to the remotest depths of our nature, and *accounts for* all its dissatisfaction with the objects of earth and time. It is Christianity alone that enables us distinctly to understand, *what it is that the heart pants for*, when it would obtain what the world cannot give us. It is Christianity alone that directs us to *the objects and ends*, in which the soul may find eternal satisfaction. And it is Christianity alone that *supplies the means*, by which these objects and ends are to be attained by us. Our religion, indeed, by the new objects of happiness which it reveals, has opened new fountains of desire in every heart that receives it. But, if it be suited to accomplish all the desires of our nature, of which, otherwise, we cannot obtain satisfaction, have we not, in this peculiarity of it, a strong indication of its truth; and a vindication, not lightly to be esteemed, of its claims upon our faith, our affections, and our lives?

It is surely a purpose, most worthy of a dispensation from God, to solve the problem, which has ever baffled, and we have reason to think, must forever have baffled the unaided reason of man, *why does disappointment, dissatisfaction, and still insatiable want, lie at the end of every effort, and of every course, in which man seeks for happiness, in the possessions, and indulgences of this world?*

Of the fact implied, no one will ask for proof. It is enough to appeal to every heart, if the most complete accomplishment that was ever obtained of earthly hope, was not soon, very soon, either followed by disappointment; or by new wants, as restless, and as clamorous as those, the satisfaction of which, it seemed, would fill up the measure of desire? Why, then, is it, that, of all the creatures of the earth, man alone has wants, which earth and time cannot satisfy? Why, when we think that we have obtained our object, does desire soon derive ten-fold enlargement from possession; or satiated with fulness, turn from it with aversion? Seek an answer to these inquiries in any other religion; and, if it teaches the doctrine of immortality, and directs the faith and hopes of its believers to another world, still, its most exalted conception of immortal felicity, is in its promise of an eternal gratification of our present senses, appetites and passions. Miserable expedient! For, what are these wants, which leave alike dissatisfied, the miser amidst his hoards, and the prodigal in his expenditures? What are these wants, which the most successful enterprise does but inflame; in the excitements of which, ambition, like the grave, never says, *it is enough;* the disappointments of which are daily seen, and felt, in the vexations and resentments, of pride and vanity; which prey upon the epicure, even while in the enjoyment of his richest banquets; and which are the torture of the sensualist, in the very fulness of what he thought would be his highest delight? Ask our religion, what are these wants? and it will tell you, that they are the admonitions of God, that this is not the place of our rest; that we were created for infinitely higher interests, and purer happiness. It will tell you, that they are at once appointments of God for our trial; and the strivings of God, to excite us to seek our happiness, where alone it can be found, *in Himself;* in the love of perfect purity, and goodness, and love; in the exercises and ends of desire, which will maintain the dominion of the higher, over the lower faculties of our nature; and which will secure to us, in the eternal improvement of these faculties,

*joys, which eye hath not seen, nor ear heard,
and which it hath not entered into the mind
of man to conceive.* See, then, how Christianity meets, and accounts for, this phenomenon in the moral condition of man! It teaches us, that these unsatisfied, and insatiable wants, arise from *our moral nature;* from that nature, which allies us to angels. It teaches us, that when we are not happy, it is because we are seeking for satisfaction, where God never intended that we should find it. It teaches us, that we cannot be happy,—that the wants of our immortal nature cannot be supplied,—till we feel, and strongly feel, our relation to the great Author of our being and affections, and fasten our desires upon Himself, as our chief good. It comes from that heaven to which it would exalt us, to breathe into every soul that will receive it, the very spirit of heaven. Say, then, if God's moral providence be not completely justified by our religion, in the disappointments, and miseries, that result from a reliance on passion, and the world,

for happiness? Will anything short of the christian's heaven, fill up the measure of our desires, and make our happiness perfect, and eternal?

My brethren, had our religion alone established the certainty of an immortal existence for man, I am ready to say, that it would have done comparatively little. But it has done, what it will not be pretended has been done, by any other religion. In the immortality which it reveals, it has provided for wants, which belong as essentially to our nature, as do hunger and thirst; which have been felt at all times; but which were never before distinctly understood, because no other religion had revealed the objects, which, by fully meeting them, had enabled those who felt, fully to explain them. They are the wants which have caused men gladly to embrace, and tenaciously to retain, even the grossest superstitions, rather than be without religion. I refer not alone to the want of a guiding wisdom, and a protecting power, superior to our own. Nor alone

to the universal desire, which has been
as unequivocally expressed, to penetrate
into the future ; to look beyond the grave ;
and, by every means to strengthen conviction, of the reality of the things hoped
for, in an eternal futurity. I refer to wants
of *the heart;* of the *affections.* I refer to
the want of an object, or of objects, which
may be forever loved, and enjoyed, undisturbed by the opposition of rival passions;
and in the possession and love of which,
we may be forever secure of that progress,
in all that can exalt our nature, the very
capacity of which, is its highest glory. I
ask, then, if our religion, by the sentiments
it gives us of God ; by the views which it
opens to us of heaven ; by the new relations into which it brings man at once to
his Maker, to his Saviour, to his fellow
creatures, and to the eternal world which
it reveals, has not given a direction to the
wants of our intellectual and moral nature,
in which, increase them in number as you
will, and enlarge each of them as you may,
every soul may obtain assurance of ultimate,

and perfect satisfaction? Yes, darkened as is the human mind by ignorance, and depraved as is the heart by sin, it is still the glory of our nature, to be capable of indefinite, and eternal improvement. And it is the glory of our religion, that it reveals to its believers a state of existence, in which all our capacities of eternal progress and happiness, may be satisfied. It most distinctly teaches us also, that the wants of our hearts, to which all the objects of this world are so disproportioned, were designed for the very end, *of raising our affections to the things that are above, where Christ sitteth at the right hand of God;* of engaging us in the cares, which concern our eternal interests; of exciting us to cultivate the principles and dispositions, and to form the character and habits, which will secure for us the approbation and love, and the eternal service and enjoyment, of God. These wants then, instead of being evidences that our nature comes corrupted from the hands of God, are his wise appointments for our trial, and preparation for a better world. Let us but feel that they belong to our immortal nature, and let us seek for the satisfaction of them, in our preparation for the christian's immortality, and in their strongest excitement, ours may be the language, and the feeling of the apostle, *as sorrowful, yet always rejoicing ; as poor, yet making many rich ; as having nothing, and yet, possessing all things.*

I cannot close this view of our subject, without a yet more distinct reference to a class of wants, for which satisfaction, or even alleviation, can be found only in religion ; and for which the gospel of Christ makes that provision, which should fill every heart with adoration and thanksgiving. I mean, the wants that are felt by an *awakened sinner.*

These are wants, which are known in some degree under every form of religion ; for they grow out of the convictions of the just desert of sin, which are felt as extensively, as the distinction is recognized between moral good and evil. But, in its new views of God, of duty, and of heaven, Christianity gives us new views of sin, and new sentiments of its deserts. And, perhaps, more has not been sustained in this world, than has been suffered by many ten thousands in Christendom, in their strong apprehensions of the judgment to come, and their conviction of just exposure to the condemnation of the impenitent. But, while our religion excites sentiments, peculiar to itself, of the guilt of disregarding, and of disobeying God; while it admonishes us, that the punishment of the obdurately wicked will be of fearful duration, and of a character to fill the heart with horror of sin; and, while it addresses every individual of mankind as a sinner, and calls every one to repentance; still, its threatenings, and every circumstance of it that is intended to impress us with the guilt, and danger, of transgressing its laws, not less even than its commands and promises, have the great design, of reclaiming us from evil; of securing our fidelity; and thus, of obtaining our *salvation*. *God has* *not appointed us unto wrath; but to obtain salvation through our Lord Jesus Christ.** The unutterably glorious doctrine of the gospel of the blessed God, is, *it is a faithful saying, and worthy of all acceptation, that Christ Jesus came into the world,* TO SAVE SINNERS.† The threatenings of the great Author of our faith, stand in our religion, as buoys placed here and there upon the shore of eternity, to admonish us of the rocks, on which, if we are wrecked, we are lost; of the whirlpools into which, if we are so far drawn as to be past recovery, our misery will be just, and inevitable. But what can an awakened sinner, who would repent and return to God, desire, which Christianity will not give to him, in its free offers of forgiveness to all who will forsake their sins; in its provision of a Mediator, an Advocate, an Intercessor for sinners; in its offers of divine assistance to us, in the work of reformation; and in the glory, with which it promises to crown

---

* Thessalonians v. 9.   † 1 Timothy i. 15.

our persevering endeavours to attain it? The blood of Christ is at once the great manifestation, and evidence, of his own love for us; and of the compassion, and readiness to pardon, of the Father who sent him. It is our sure pledge, that not one hope, that is justified by his promises, will ever be disappointed. Has not Christianity, then, combined in its character, all that can commend it to our *reason*, to our *affections*, and to our *wants?*

In some of its means, in regard to the universal dominion at which it aims, the religion of Christ is indeed a scheme, as yet but imperfectly comprehended by man. It is to receive new, and greatly important illustration, from events, the time, and manner of accomplishing which, are known only to God. As it is now seen in the world, it is obscured by idle, and presumptuous speculations; corrupted by the additions which human ignorance has made to it; perverted by prejudices; opposed by evil passions; and abused to the very purposes, which it would utterly repress in every heart. We see it, broken up into sects; and assuming as many forms, and distinctive traits of character, as have the great parties, into which Christendom is divided. So, it may be, it has yet long to suffer. But, let us be animated by the assurance, that it will overpower all resistance, scatter all darkness, subdue all evil passions, and fill the earth with the knowledge, and the glory of God. Let this conviction be our confidence; and, in the strength of it, let us watch and pray, that we may ourselves be found worthy in the day of the Lord. Sooner will heaven and earth pass away, than one word will fail which our God and Father has spoken unto us by his Son.

This, my friends, is the religion, that claims the ministry, which we have this day established here, according to the institution of Christ. Ours is, therefore, emphatically, *a ministry of reconciliation.* It is a part of that glorious economy, by which God is designing to renew the moral world; to make every heart a temple of his holy spirit; to prepare his moral off-spring on earth, for immortal felicity in heaven. I hardly need to say then, what the Christian Ministry *should be;* what it *must be*, in order to the accomplishment of its unspeakably important ends.

The model of a minister of Jesus should be, *Jesus himself.* Let us then, in the exercise of our ministry, look always to him as our great example. To a great extent, Christianity is still struggling against the same passions, and the same interests, which it had to resist in the days of our Lord, and his apostles; and its claims upon us can be satisfied by nothing less, than the devotion of our whole hearts, and our whole lives, to its objects; by a purity of character, an activity of benevo-lence, and a never ceasing zeal, in which it shall be *seen*, and *felt*, that the spiritual good, the greatest christian improvement, and the eternal salvation of those for whom we are appointed to labour, are always paramount in our minds. It claims of us, that we watch for souls as they that must give account. It claims of us, that deep feeling of the greatness, and the holiness of its objects, which will make us willing to spend, and to be spent in its service; which will make us instant in season, and out of season; which will make us alive to God, through Jesus Christ; alive to the feeling, that he who converteth a sinner from the errour of his ways, will save a soul from death, and hide a multitude of sins. Do we feel that we are but poor, feeble, unworthy instruments? So should we feel, to excite us continually to seek our sufficiency from God; for indeed, without him, we are nothing. But, blessed will be that servant, whom his Lord, when he cometh, shall find so doing!

My dear friend and brother,

Deeply affected as I know you are, with a sense of the responsibility of the office with which you are this day invested, I hardly need to urge upon you the claims of our religion. But, you cannot feel them too strongly. You cannot have them too constantly before you. Favourable as are the circumstances, under which you enter upon the ministry in this place, you will find that, for the attainment of its objects, all the solicitude of your heart will be demanded; all the earnestness, and vigilance, and labour, of which you are capable. To satisfy these claims, let your application be incessant to the Source of all wisdom, for guidance, and for strength. If you will be a faithful minister, you will have difficulties to encounter, not altogether unlike those of the master, to whom you have given yourself. May the distinctive character of our religion be faithfully maintained in your preaching, and illustrated in your life! May you be the honoured instrument of bringing many, to the faith and obedience of the Son of God; of bringing many to glory, and honour, and immortality! Be faithful to every individual. Be faithful unto death. And, may the Lord give you the reward of a faithful servant!

Brethren of this religious society,

You have this day acknowledged one of the great claims of our religion, in the establishment you have made of the ministry which it has appointed. But permit me to say to you, that the demands of Christianity extend far beyond the maintainance of its ordinances. Its demands are as great, even as its promises. It claims the best exercise of your reason upon its doctrines, and its duties ; upon its immediate and its final purposes. It claims, not only an interest in your affections, but the possession of them ; the unreserved control of all their exercises. It claims the renovation of your heart from all that is unchristian in it ; your entire subjection to the will of God in Christ Jesus concerning you ; and your faithful improvement, under a sense of your responsibility for them, of all the means of forming a christian character, and of preparation for an inheritance of the christian's reward. If the world is to be made better than it now is ; if vice is to be corrected, knowledge promoted, character raised, and happiness advanced, it must be by the extension of the influence of our religion; and it is a law of God's moral providence, that each one who believes the gospel, should act in the cause of its advancement. Acknowledge then, my friends, and satisfy its claims, by an unreserved dedication of yourselves to God, through his Son; by the consecration to him of your families; by your daily prayers, and ready efforts, and cheerful sacrifices, for the interests of the church; by cultivating enlarged christian sympathies; and by your supreme regard to God's acceptance, in every desire, and in every pursuit of life. In these claims of our religion, see the ends of its ministry. They are the interests of your everlasting life with God, and Christ, and holy spirits in heaven. In the services of this house, may you, and may our children, find increasing light, and strength, and encouragement, and comfort, and peace! May you have cause to look back with gratitude on the transactions of this hour, when you shall stand at

the judgment seat of Christ ; and may the
ministry of this our beloved brother, be to
you for exceeding joy, through the ages of
eternity!

AMEN!

THE CHARGE,

BY REV. JAMES KENDALL,

OF PLYMOUTH.

MY DEAR BROTHER,

You have already devoted yourself, and you have this day been publicly consecrated by prayer and the imposition of hands to the sacred work of the Christian Ministry. You are now to receive the Charge from the Churches, which we represent. We claim by this service no dominion of your faith. We make no pretension to any authority to communicate spiritual or miraculous gifts, or powers. We assume no superiority of rights or privileges. We are not of the number, nor, we trust, of the temper and character of those who would say to any religious denomination, or to any individual christian, Stand by thyself; come not nigh unto us; for we are holier than thou. One is our Master, even Christ: And one is our Father, who is in heaven; and all we are brethren.

But as elder brethren, who have laboured a little longer in the faith and patience of Jesus Christ, we may be permitted to remind you of some of the duties, which from your pastoral office will devolve upon you; the trials to which you may be called; and the temper and character necessary and proper for you to cherish and maintain, in order to discharge acceptably these duties, and endure as becometh a servant of the Lord the trials that await you. What we have to suggest on this occasion is implied in the Apostolic injunction;—Take heed to thyself; and to thy doctrine; and to the flock over which the Churches by the authority of the Holy Ghost, have now made thee an overseer. In the spirit and language of this inspired injunction, therefore, and with the sympathies of brethren, you will bear with us, while we intreat and charge thee to

Take heed to thyself. Not only your personal satisfaction and comfort, but your success and usefulness as a religious teacher and the good influence of your example will greatly depend, under God, on the attention you pay to your own heart and life. No man, whatever may be the station he is called to fill, can hope to be respected and honoured by others, if he feel no respect for, and pay no regard to himself. But the office you now hold is a sacred and an elevated one. It ought, therefore, to be magnified; and magnified by cultivating the christian temper; by cherishing and manifesting a christian spirit, and by portraying to the life the christian character. You are a city set upon a hill for the world to gaze at, for curiosity to pry into, and for bigotry and fanaticism to sit in judgment upon. Take heed that it be not stained by moral defilement; that it be not disfigured by any fictitious ornament; that there be nothing either within or without that shall offend the eye or the taste of the most pure and pious observer. Never suffer your mind to be corrupted from the simplicity that is in Christ. Sanctify the Lord God in your heart;—having a good conscience, that, whereas they should speak evil of you, as of an evil doer, they may be ashamed that falsely accuse your good conversation in Christ. Keep thyself pure. Let no man despise thee.

To the purity and dignity that belong to the pastoral office, add the meekness and humility, the gentleness and condescension, that were exemplified by our great High Priest, who has passed into the heavens. Beware of that austerity of manner and that gloominess of deportment, which would leave the impression, that religion must never be named nor "approached, but with an altered tone, and a disfigured face." Let it be seen by your own example, that there is nothing forbidding in her attire, nothing stern, but to profligacy and vice, in her address ; nothing unsocial in her intercourse with mankind. There may be cheerfulness without levity, and sobriety without moroseness. If you put on the Lord Jesus Christ you will be clothed with humility, and your adorning will be that of the hidden man of the heart, even the ornament of a meek and quiet spirit, which in the sight of God is of great price. Perfect yourself in that most important gift, an aptness to teach, connected with patience and meekness in instructing those who are slow to learn, and slower to believe, resisting the truth and opposing themselves. Keep the example of Christ always before you, and follow his steps. If you are reviled, learn of him not to revile again. If you are called to suffer for righteousness' or truth's sake, threaten not; but commit yourself and the cause to Him who judgeth righteously. Be thou an example of the believers in word, in conversation, in charity, in spirit, in faith, in purity.

Again, take heed to thy doctrine. Let your instructions be drawn from the fountain of light and truth, the revelation of God. Employ all the means with which you are favoured, and all the powers you possess for coming unto the knowledge of the truth. Endeavour to discriminate between what is taught by the inspiration of God, and those corrupt appendages, which ignorance, or prejudice, or superstition has incorporated with it; between what was applicable to the condition and circumstances of the people in the time of the apostles, and what was designed to apply to mankind in all ages. Beware of teaching for doctrine the commandments of men. Let the word of God be the standard, and test, and limit of your religious inquiries. Be not wise above what is written. But imagine not that the science of theology alone, of all the sciences, has come to a stand: That while the human mind is advancing and improving in every other region of thought, no further progress is to be made in searching out the treasures of wisdom and knowledge, that are laid up in the gospel: That all the light and truth contained in the sacred volume were unfolded and imparted to the uninspired men, who lived in the darkest and most corrupt age of the christian church. Spiritual light like the natural, shineth brighter and brighter unto the perfect day. If therefore you would grow in grace and in the knowledge of our Lord and Saviour Jesus Christ, keep your mind open to all the light and truth that shall at any time break forth from the written word of God.* Omit no doctrine merely because it is old, and keep back none because it appears to be new, provided it be found in the word, and taught by the authority of God, and be necessary and profitable for instruction in righteousness, and for perfecting your charge in the christian temper and life. Aim to make your hearers wise, and good, and happy, rather than able disputants or expert theologians. Be more solicitous to impart light to their understandings, and grace and truth to

* See Mr. Robinson's charge to the Plymouth Church.

their hearts, than to entertain them with unintelligible or enigmatical propositions, which you are unable to explain, and they to comprehend. The way of holiness is represented as an highway, so plain and so direct, that way-faring men, though fools, need not err therein. Let all your preaching, therefore, have a practical tendency, that your hearers may be made perfect, thoroughly furnished unto every good work. We do not charge you to preach the doctrines of the Reformation any farther than you find them, on a careful examination to accord with the word of God. But we do enjoin upon you to adhere without wavering or doubting to the great principles of Protestantism, the sufficiency of the holy scriptures, and the right of private judgment in the interpretation of them. The authority of God the Father, and of Jesus Christ the Son of the Father, is paramount to all other authority; and the doctrine delivered by the anointed Son and Messenger of the most high God, ought to be declared by his ministering servants, whether mankind hear, or whether they forbear. Every ambassador of Jesus Christ, as well as every other rational being, must give an account of himself and of his stewardship to God. He must be saved by his own faith, and not by the faith of his brethren. It is, therefore, a right and privilege, which the author of his being has given him, to judge of himself what the word of God teaches, and be fully persuaded in his own mind, if he would know and declare all the counsel of God. This right we charge you to claim and maintain, as being alone accountable to the God of truth for the exercise of it; and never to demand of others a sacrifice, which your Lord does not require of you. Never render applicable to yourself the pointed interrogatory of the apostle: Who art thou that judgeth another man's servant? To his own Master he standeth or falleth. Stand fast, therefore, in the liberty wherewith Christ hath made us free; and be not entangled again in the yoke of bondage.

Once more: Take heed to the flock over which thou art placed as an overseer. Watch over it with the vigilance, and kindness, and tenderness of the good Shepherd. Feed the sheep, and feed the lambs. Feed them with food adapted to their respective age and character; but always with knowledge and understanding. Let your doctrine drop as the rain, and your speech distil as the dew. Beware lest they substitute something for religion, in which it has little or no concern. There is no substitute for personal righteousness or holiness. Press upon them the consideration, that without rational faith, and sincere repentance, and obedience to the truth, there is no acceptance with God— no ground to hope for an interest in the forgiving mercy of heaven. The design of christianity, and of all our Lord did and taught, and suffered, was to bless mankind in turning them away from their iniquities. If this design be accomplished in them, the blessing is secured. But, if this benevolent purpose of God be frustrated through their own perverseness, they will fail of an interest in his grace, and forfeit the promised blessing.

With regard to christian ordinances, they are to be administered to the proper subjects; and of their qualifications for the enjoyment of these ordinances you are to be the judge. But take heed that you do not set up any condition for admission to these ordinances, which are not warranted by the word of God. In nothing perhaps, have the churches more widely departed from apostolic practice, than in what relates to the observance of the ordinances of the gospel. Too much has been required by those within, and too little regard paid to these ordinances by those without the pale of the church. The christian world, with respect to them, seem to have lost sight of the simplicity that there is in Christ. The ordinance of baptism, we think, is to be administered to believers and their infant seed; and to be administered on the profession of the parents' faith in the Son of God. This is the outward sign or token of their covenant relation to God. It introduces them into the school of Christ, where they are taught to observe all things whatsoever he has commanded. The Lord's Supper is among the means of building them up in faith and holiness, and fitting them for the enjoyment of the saints' inheritance in light; and is to be administered to all who believe in him as the promised Messiah, the anointed Son of God; who appear to love him in sincerity; and who desire to do whatsoever he has commanded. Beyond this, we have no authority, and can exercise no judgment; but must leave the rest to the great Searcher of hearts, who has appointed a day and the method for separating the tares from the wheat, and assigning to each their respective portion.

In presiding in the church, the apostolic injunction is, not to lord it over God's heritage. The servant of the Lord must not strive, but be gentle to all men. Reclaim the wanderer, and them that are out of the way, if possible, by kindness and tenderness, and a due consideration of their weaknesses, and frailties, and temptations. Break not the bruised reed. Quench not the almost expiring taper. But, where the vital spark is not extinguished, carefully nourish, and feed, and rekindle it to a flame—not a flame that will consume; but warm, and cheer, and comfort. Be wise to win souls.

And the things that thou hast heard of us among many witnesses, the same commit thou to faithful men, who shall be able to teach others also. Lay hands suddenly on no man. And do not hastily defraud a people of their rights by withholding your sanction from the man of their choice, and peradventure, a man after God's own heart. Insist not as a condition of your countenance and assistance in the settlement of a young minister, on an explicit avowal of those abstruse, speculative opinions, which have long divided the christian world, and about the correctness of which, the ablest and best divines, who have laboured longest in the pursuit of truth, have been less confident at the close, than at the commencement of their inquiries. If there be competent abilities and qualifications for the sacred work, and a heart devoted to the service of God, with a determination to follow the path of light and truth marked out by the gospel, bid him God speed, and let him go on his way, diligent in the pursuit of christian knowledge, and rejoicing in the discovery of christian truth.

And now, my brother, be strong in the Lord and in the power of his might. Be of good courage, and he shall strengthen thine heart. Watch thou in all things; endure afflictions; do the work of an evangelist; make full proof of thy Ministry. And when the time of your departure is at hand, may you be able in the language of victory and triumph to say, *I have fought a good fight, I have finished my course, I have kept the faith; henceforth there is laid up for me a crown of righteousness, which the Lord, the righteous Judge shall give me at that day.*

RIGHT HAND OF FELLOWSHIP.

BY REV. SAMUEL J. MAY,

OF BROOKLYN, CONN.

———

You are now, my Brother, regularly inducted to the Gospel Ministry. It is not pretended that by Ordination any mysterious gifts are conferred; but this is not therefore an unmeaning ceremony. The design of Ordination is, to impress deeply upon the pastor and his flock, the important purposes and corresponding duties of their union, thus publicly solemnized. As high as heaven is above the earth, so high are the objects, which this union contemplates, above all secular concerns. The relation of ministers and people is, beyond any other, holy, solemn, tender. It is spiritual. It has nothing to do with sense and time, but to counteract their influence. It has nothing to do with the passions and evil propensities of men, but to subject them to the laws of God. It is a relation, the influence of which, on character and happiness, will remain, when the world shall be no more.

By the connexion you have now formed with this people, your and their eternal interests will be deeply affected. They have chosen you to be their Pastor, trusting that you will "nourish them with substantial and salutary food; that you will lead them into green pastures and beside the still waters, and not to thirsty plains or the barren wilderness." They have put themselves under you as their guide, trusting that you know the way to eternal life. What a trust! Should you be unfaithful, my brother, how apalling the consequences will be! In shame and confusion you will stand before the great Shepherd, with the flock he has committed to your charge, famished and unfit to be admitted into his fold.

It is the part of brotherly love thus to put you in remembrance of these things, (though you know them) that you may stir up all the gifts of God which are in you, to the faithful discharge of the ministry you have received. And now that, in behalf of this Council, I give you the Right Hand of Fellowship, I do it as a pledge that we will continue to shew you this and other proofs of our brotherly love. We request from you a return of the same. We claim no pre-eminence, no authority over you. You are entirely our equal. Christ only is our master; all we are brethren ; and we need each others counsel and aid, and sympathy, and prayers. What should make us thus "kindly affectioned," one to another, if not the nature, the importance and the difficulties of the work, in which we are fellow-labourers. Shall we who are to herald forth that gospel, which proclaims peace on earth, good will to men, shall we be unfriendly, contentious? We, who are to teach a religion, whose essence is love, shall we have none of that spirit, which suffereth long, and is kind? We, who have engaged to defend and to forward that cause in which Christ died, shall we allow differences of opinion on points of minor consequence to alienate our affections, produce dissension, and by dividing, enfeeble our efforts, all of which united would be scarcely worthy their object? O! what disgrace has already been brought upon the name we bear! How has Christ been put to open shame, yes, crucified afresh by the sectarism and bigotry of his professed disciples! Those doctrines, about which Christians have ever been divided, are allowed even by their warmest advocates to be mysterious; that is to say, not fully revealed. If then God, who is infinitely wise and good, has seen fit to leave these subjects still in obscurity, "what high presumption, what a rude encroachment on the province of God it is" for one man to dictate to another what he is to believe respecting them! Yet such has been, and such still is the presumption of many fallible mortals. Excommunication and anathema have been hurled at those who have dared, however impelled by conviction, to dissent from the popular faith ; and he has lived in a happy age, or a happy country who, guilty of such offence, has escaped the dungeon, the rack or the faggot. It is on different principles, the principles of Protestant liberty—it is with the acknowledgment of our common fallibility, and with the purpose of mutual improvement, that we welcome you to the liberal studies as well as the arduous labours of our holy profession. We welcome you not as the dictators, but as the helpers and partners of your faith and joy. We "bid you God speed" in the sacred paths of religious inquiry and christian duty. Go on then, following "the Bible, the Bible only" as your guide, however it may lead you to dissent from the confessions of Assemblies and the systems of those who have denominated half the christian world. What is it to you and me, that Calvin and Socinus believed one thing or another? The great inquiry with us is, what doth Christ teach? and we should be so absorbed in this inquiry, that it would be pardonable in us to forget that Calvin and Socinus ever lived. They were, it is true, great men, and deserve our respect, but cannot claim any submission to their authority. They were no more than men, imperfect, fallible men, liable to be warped by prejudice, to be blinded by passion, and driven to extremes. Besides which, they lived at the time when Christianity was just awaking from the slumber of ages. That long, dark night was not dispelled at once by a morning of unclouded brightness. Ignorance and superstition were not succeeded at once by correct views of God and religion. No—very much is yet to be done before "the truth as it is in Jesus," unadulterated by any human admixtures, will prevail in the world. But there is a vast deal more knowledge in the present age than there was at the period of the Reformation. Then, the Scriptures were just brought to light. Ever since then, they have been the subject of more research and profound investigation than any or all other books. Ought we therefore to go back three hundred years to Calvin and Socinus and inquire what these scriptures teach? This surely would be the height of folly, unless we believe they were inspired men. We have no reason to believe this. Therefore let us not assent implicitly or too readily to their opinions. But let us gladly avail ourselves of the labours of the wise and good at and since the time of the Reformation, and in the light of their researches, let us press on to the simple and majestic truth.

In this glorious pursuit, we ought each to encourage and animate the other, by freely communicating the results of our own study and reflection. We should thus afford reciprocal aid in the detection of errour and the solution of difficulties. Why should there be the least reserve or jealousy on this subject? An amicable discussion would often result in mutual concessions and a union of sentiment. Discussion always will be amicable when we duly respect each others rights. Let us then never, my brother, never for a moment indulge the wish to coerce assent to our opinions. Though we may feel sure they are correct, we may be mistaken. Others, wiser and better than we are, have been thus mistaken, and surely he is deluded, who deems himself exempt from the frailties incident to humanity. As brethren, we may and ought to point out and endeavour to rectify each others errours; but this should always be done in the spirit of charity, which thinketh no evil. and in the spirit of meekness, remembering that we also may often err.

Having very lately myself experienced the solemn impressions and tender solicitude, which are awakened by an occasion like this, I do sympathise with you sincerely. We have commenced, my brother, the most important era of our lives. We have entered into the most solemn engagements; and the labours, the trials and responsibilities that lie before us, seem to say "who is sufficient for these things?" Let us be fervent in spirit, for we are to serve the Lord. Let us be instant in prayer, for we need his grace. God is ever near and ever ready to enlighten our ignorance, to strengthen our weakness, and to have mercy upon us. Amidst the trials and privations to which we may be called in this world of darkness and sin, let us not faint or be weary in well doing, for we shall soon leave this for that far better world, where pure and kindred spirits will be happily united forever; where we shall be continually advancing to perfection; where prejudice and passion will not mislead us; where we shall see what here we cannot see, and know what here we cannot know; where we shall pursue our contemplations without interruption or perplexity; where we shall reason without errour, and labour without fatigue.